if it ain't one thing it's another

A NOVEL BY
SHARRON DOYLE

Copyright 2007 by Sharron Doyle
ISBN: 097594536X

Edited by Leah Whitney
Design/Photogaphy: Jason Claiborne

First printing Augustus Publishing paperback May 2007

AUGUSTUS
PUBLISHING

AugustusPublishing.com
33 Indian Road New York, New York 10034

ACKNOWLEDGEMENTS

To my Blood fam: Mom, we did it! I love you to death lady, And I pray that my accomplishment makes you smile for all the years I made you sad.

To my first cousin Cherie I hope you enjoy reading as much as I enjoyed writing

Parkeya I'm so proud of you, Pooda. College girl, keep doing big things – Remember what I told you many moons ago – education is gangsta. I love you.

Chale and Tashiem I pray that neither of you make the mistakes that I made in my growing years. Know that I lived it for you and I've done the research, so that you never have to. Stay focused, stay directed and like always – stay in school. Love you to death won't let no trouble come your way.

To Charmainne and Deshaun may Allah bless y'all with endless happiness and Charma keep striving.

To my cuzzo Rasham (Boobie) I love you and pray that you have the world in your hands. Stay up!

To my street fam: B.J. the streets is yours my neezie. I don't care how old you get – you still my baby boy. Curtis you pretty boy uptown's cutest. Doreen, I told you I want to grow up and be just like you :). Ladelle and Tutu y'all give meaning to the word "gangsta". Lou Dingo make the bitches wanna purr! You know I know. Monique "Booga" Gary and John "Fix It" Powell, thank you for being there during my dark days. My appreciation goes a lifetime.

Leon I can never thank you enough for standing by me through all my bids and bull-shit. You are stuck with me for life.

Maleek and Raheem on 140th – thanks for keeping dough in my pocket.

To the old-timers on 143rd, Ms. Cherbin, Brother and Pope

your warm hellos and greetings always put a smile on my face. Thank you for not judging me.

Joyce "Juice" Copeland you know the love I have for you is eternal. I want nothing but the best for you. Gangestress, stay up.

To my Casat sistas who encouraged me to keep writing and to keep hope alive. Rachelle Venable you are one of the loyalest women I know and I pray that I can get up wit' you again. I love you Sissy and you helped me to stay hungry in this game.

Joyce Sanders my hopes go out to you and yours that your struggles are few and your victories are many.

Wendy Dupree when its all said and done I'll get up wit' you in da town. Thank you for being a dedicated reader on this novel and arts 2 and 3. Your laughter made me want to write more.

To the rest of my Casat sistas who read the book when it was on lined paper and urged me to hurry up, because ya'll wanted more – I love ya'll to death. Katrina Houser, Janice Jenkins, Tracy Ligon, Tasheema McNeil and India Scott. I pray that we never see each other behind the wall again. I wish all you ladies the best.

Ms. Tucker thank you for the work that you put in on this project in your spare time. I wish you a peaceful journey in your recovery.

Mr. Carter in the law library thanks for allowing me to use the typewriter, when all the other officers were hatin'. I appreciate that.

To all the peeps behind the wall stay up and do something positive wit' your time.

Last but far from least I wanna give a xxtra special thanks to Anthony White and Jason Claiborne. Dam, I don't even know where to start. :)J. First 'nuff thanxs for puttin' me on and letting me get my feet wet. I owe you guys everything for introducing me to the world of urban fiction. Wow, I'm getting teary eyed..... Jason, thank you for doin' the damn thing on the cover and the bookmarks. You said it would happen and it has.

Anthony, thank you so much for being tolerant wit' me through all my immature outbursts. I guess you understood what I was goin' through. Thanks for not abandoning me.

Leah Whitfield I extend my gratitude to you for doing the editing and also exercising a lot of tolerance wit' me. Thank you for letting me understand what the word "change" means in editing dialogue.

To anybody I missed put your name here _____.

To all the readers I know that you will enjoy this novel. Get at me through Augustus Publishing and know that this is Part 1 of a trilogy. Look for Part 2 "When Love Turns to Hate" and Part 3 "Good Things Gone Bad", coming soon to a hood near you.

One Million,
Sharron

Thanks to the Augustus Manuscript Team for their tireless work and contributions in making my dream a reality. Thanks to Leah Whitney Tamiko Maldonado, Yasmin Sangari,

Check us at the website **Augustuspublishing.com** Go hard or go home, One.

PROLOGUE

Share had just left a meeting and was on her way home. Luther Vandross was pumping from the speakers of her brand new Lexus. She'd had a long day and was now ready for some woodwork, which always released the day's pressure.

Share was dark-skinned with deep dimples, a beautiful set of teeth and high cheekbones. She could have been a supermodel if she chose. Instead she was a single businesswoman with no kids.

Share turned onto her block and parked. She grabbed her briefcase off the passenger's seat and went into the house. She started to ring Petie's phone to tell him to come now, but she decided not to. He'd probably get there late, but he'd be there. She undressed, put on some music, turned on the shower and got in.

chapter
one

Share had just stepped out of the shower and was drying off when the phone rang. It was Petie. He was calling to let her know that he was on his way. Petie was a chocolate brotha with a six pack, a bunch of tattoos and a big dick. Yeah, he had a big gun. Share liked that.

She kept her feelings in check when it came to him or any other nigga. *Niggas ain't shit but money and dick. Get on your knees and suck my clit.* That was her motto, so catching feelings was a no-no.

Share remembered that she didn't douche. She had a variety of scents to choose from in her Summer's Eve selection: baby powder, vinegar and water, mountain rain and floral. She decided on mountain rain. She opened it up and swoosh-swoosh. She always

felt good after a douche. *Keep that booty hole fresh, girl*, she said to herself.

Share went into the bedroom and smoothed White Diamonds lotion all over her body and then sprayed some between her legs. *Fresh just for you, baby boy.* She knew Petie would be there any minute, ready to beat it up. Just thinking about it made her body jump. She had a heartbeat down there and he hadn't even arrived yet. *Damn, I'm open... slow down, breathe easy and remember he's only a play thing.* She'd told herself that a number of times, but her body just wouldn't listen.

Petie called Share again to let her know that he had just parked the truck and to come downstairs and open the door for him. She'd thought about giving him keys, but she knew that would be the worst thing to do. That nigga would really think he was the boss if she did that. She let him be the boss in the bedroom; that was good enough.

Share didn't take orders or demands from anybody; she was the boss. But there was something about Petie that made her weak. And she was scared of her feelings when it came to him. He was only her back-breaker, she kept telling herself. That was it and that was all. But her emotions kept making her feel otherwise.

She knew he would be downstairs by now, so she threw on a spandex cat suit along with her favorite animal slippers and ran downstairs. Petie liked to see her in a cat suit, and he particularly liked the front, where it would cut between her pussy lips. Share had fat lips on her chocolate box, and right now she was ready for him to suck her sweets.

Petie waited patiently on the steps of Share's brownstone. She opened the door and stepped back into the foyer to let him in, and he gave her a pretty-ass smile that said, "You know I'm about to beat it." She loved that smile. And she knew all of his looks and what they meant too. She also knew she would have to dead it before he hurt her; Petie was a heartbreaker who was not gonna leave his wife.

"What I told you about having me downstairs waiting like that? You know parole is looking for me," Petie said when they got upstairs.

"Baby, please, the warrant squad ain't out at night, so be easy," Share replied.

"Yeah, aiight." Petie took off his coat, threw it on a chair in the living room and made two drinks for them. She knew he liked to drink and argue before he got at her. He was on it like that. He would think of something to be angry about and then take it out on her in bed. She liked that rough shit, and she did all the things wifey did-n't do. That's why his ass kept coming back.

The phone on her nightstand in the bedroom rang, and before Share could go and answer it, Petie rushed by her and snatched it up. "Speak. Who dis?" he barked. Petie waited impa-tiently for a few seconds to find out who was calling. Then he said, "Yeah, well, she's busy." And that was all Share heard before he pulled the phone's cord out of the wall. *Here we go. Now he's got something to be angry about*, she thought. "Come up out of that cat suit!" Petie called out before ordering her into the bedroom.

Petie placed his drink on the nightstand as Share entered the bedroom. The first thing she noticed was the phone on the floor.

She stepped out of her cat suit and picked up the phone. Seeing the plug disconnected from the jack she said, "What the fuck you do to my phone?" Petie didn't answer. He had taken off his shirt and was coming out of his jeans now, giving her a 'You know what time it is' look. Damn, she loved that look. *This nigga...ah, man, I'm feeling his gangsta,* she thought. Share never let Petie know how she truly felt about him, because then he would fuck everything up.

"Oh, you don't hear me now? I said, what the fuck you do to my phone?"

"Nothing!" Petie pulled out the K-Y Jelly andbegan stroking himself. "Who the fuck is Will?" he finally said.

"A friend—and stop answering my phone. I don't answer *your* phone—do I? All right then." She knew the more shit she popped the more intense their encounter would be, so she kept poppin' shit. And the more shit she popped the harder his dick got.

"You feeling brave tonight, huh...comin' out ya face. You gangsta now, huh?" Petie said.

Share kept on and on. She got up in his grill, talking more shit. "Yeah, nigga, I'm feelin' gangsta—now what? Get it crunk!" she said, and he did. Before she could go on, Petie was biting her on the neck. He turned her around and started smacking his dick between her cheeks. He spit on her bumper and rubbed it on her hole. He called it his *goodness.* "Ma, gimme my goodness," he'd say. But tonight he was taking it. It was all right, though. He could do that; it was his. Share never let anybody else hit her there. Petie rubbed his fingers around her entry, massaging the hole. Every now and then he would stick his tongue inside, just to get her more ready.

Petie was so smooth and despite his large sized penis, he never ripped her. And he always talked her through it. "Share, put your thumb in your mouth," he said. "Yeah, like that. Now relax, ma, daddy got you. Don't run from me. Open up and let me in...yeah, that's what's up. Gimme my goodness."

She felt him moving in deeper. "Ooh, God, Petie...please," she moaned. The head was the worst part, but once that got in it was a wrap. Share was on the floor on all fours with her back arched, her bumper at Petie's waist level. But the more he pushed, the lower she got. He continued stroking, and her butt began making juices, allowing him to easily slide in and out of her.

Share climbed onto the bed and Petie followed, hitting her like he was on a hang glider. He was giving her full pressure now, and it was his turn to pop shit. "So who the fuck is Will, huh?" stroking her deeper each time he asked.

"Aaah, Petie, please wait. Be nice," Share begged.

"Tell Will to lose your number, ya heard?" he said digging his gun deeper into her hole.

Oh, God, help me, Share thought. She couldn't take it any-more. It felt like he was making a new hole that wasn't supposed to be there. She fell flat on her stomach, hoping his gun would slip out—it didn't. Petie was long and strong and when she fell, he fell right with her; there was no escaping...in and out, in and out.

Share began to cry out. Petie loved that shit. The more she cried and moaned, the harder he stroked her. She just didn't know that all that crying made his dick even harder.

"Share, be quiet. Why are you making me punish you like

6

this, huh? Answer me, ma." He was taunting her now. If she didn't answer right away he would go even deeper, and Share knew it.

"I don't know. I'm sorry," she whined. He stroked her long and easy now. He spread her bumper cheeks so he could slide his whole self inside her. "Aaah, God, Petie...please, please."

"Please what, ma? Huh, please what? Answer me." Before Share could respond, she was coming all over the place. Her pussy cat was soaking wet; it was like a waterfall. *God, this nigga is gonna make me crazy,* she thought.

Petie's breathing quickened and he was stroking her long and hard again. He re-applied pressure, this time creating smacking noises each time he thrust himself inside of her. He pulled out and thrust himself back into her over and over again, until he finally fell on top of her, out of breath and kissing the back of her neck. "Whew! That's what's up, ma," he said. He rolled off of her, gave her a long kiss, wiped the sweat off her face and then kissed her nose. Share turned over onto her back, crossed her legs and looked over at Petie. After a few moments she got up, grabbed her hairbrush from off the dresser and swept her hair back; Petie had sweated out her doobie.

Share walked to the living room and took Petie's phone out of his coat pocket. She checked the missed calls to see if she recognized any of the numbers. *Ha!* Wifey had called only about three hundred times. She wished she knew his password so she could hear the messages. *Don't worry; I'm sending him home now, bitch,* she thought. She hated the idea of him leaving to go home to her. She wondered if he dug wifey out the same way he did her. The thought made her sick. She knew who his wife was, but his wife didn't know who she was. She put the phone back in his pocket after erasing all of the missed calls. He didn't need to know that she'd called so many times. Shit, he was *going home* to her.

Share fixed herself a drink and sat on the couch naked, waiting for Petie to come out of the bedroom. She thought that maybe they could swing another episode. Petie walked into the living room putting on his shirt. He looked at Share, wanting to get at her again, but there was no more time for that now; he knew wifey had probably blown his phone up. He bent down in front of Share, spread her legs and sucked on her sweets. She wrapped her legs around his neck, and he nibbled and licked on her clitoris until she was fully arched. He finally gave her one last suck before getting up and kissing her long and deep, their tongues entwined. "Next time, ma," Petie said kissing her nose. He reached for his coat and let himself out of the apartment. Share threw on a robe and ran downstairs to watch him walk to his truck. *Yeah, next time, baby boy*, she thought. *Damn, I'm caught up with this nigga*. Share's emotions were all over the place. *It'll be all right...next time*.

chapter TWO

Petie jumped in his truck and grabbed DMX's *It's Dark and Hell Is Hot* CD. He popped it into his CD player and pulled off, with *How's It Goin' Down* pumping out of his speakers. He always played that before and after seeing Share.

Petie knew Share was whipped. He put it on all the chicks like that. Nobody was special—not even wifey. He only stayed with her because of the kids. She was home base. Nobody could touch that, and he refused to let it go. She took care of his sons and cooked meals every night. Nah, he wasn't going anywhere. What wifey didn't know wouldn't hurt her. But if it wasn't for his sons he would've *been* bounced. She wasn't fun in the bedroom anymore. She was boring—unlike Share. Share was creative and always willing, and she took it in the bumper. Yeah, that's what he liked. Share was his, and if he ever found out somebody else was hitting that, he'd beat her down. However, there'd be none of that; he knew she enjoyed that bedroom punishment. But if he ever caught her cheating, there'd be no enjoyment whatsoever—believe that.

Petie checked his phone and was surprised to see that wifey didn't call. That was strange. He pulled up to his building, shut the system off and hopped out of the truck. The regular cats were out front, waiting for the heads to come through. That's how it was in the hood—always on the paper chase. Family gotta eat, bills gotta be paid and muthafuckas don't want to hire convicted felons.... Get that money; it's yours for the taking.

Petie put the key in the door, hoping that wifey would be asleep. But something told him she'd be up waiting for him with a million questions. He walked into his sons' bedroom and looked in on them. They were fast asleep...his little men. He loved them to death. That's what kept him coming home every night.

Petie took off his coat and went to the bedroom to see if his wife, Renee, was awake. She was. She gave him a 'Where you been?' look. He pulled off his G-Units and lined them up with the other twenty-six pairs of kicks he had. Petie had different footwear for every day of the month. You name it, he had it, and he made sure his little men had it too.

Petie kissed Renee on the cheek, and she began with the million questions. "Where you been? Why didn't you call? Why you look like that? Why you always gotta go out at night? What took you so long? Who was you with? Was you with a bitch? Why you lyin'?" *Damn, she's nosy*. He wanted to be rid of her ass, but he wouldn't

do that to his sons. Renee was a good mother. He couldn't take that away from her. She had homemaker skills. She took care of the house and devoted all of her time to their sons. He couldn't break up his happy home.

Petie remembered growing up and watching his mother struggle and work two jobs to make ends meet. She had a hard life, and he always wondered as a boy why his father just upped and left the way he did. He thought his pops didn't love him. Petie remembered how unwanted and neglected he felt as a child without his father...all the other kids doing things with their dads and his was nowhere around. He had abandoned him and left him to grow up without him. He hated him for that, and he vowed that he would never cause his little men that kind of pain—never; so if it meant that he was stuck with Renee for life, then so be it. He was determined to have his sons grow up with both of their parents. He lived for them since they were born. They were all that mattered...his little men. But here he was being interrogated again, as usual. It was a no-win situation.

Petie snatched off his clothes down to his boxers and got in the bed. He took the remote control and turned on some porno. He had to watch the porno channel just to get in the mood to be with Renee. It just wasn't the same anymore; she no longer excited him, so he would watch the chicks on the screen and imagine that he was hitting them instead.... Damn, one chick looked like Desiree...yeah, Des. Petie was thinking about going to check her tomorrow. She was a head nurse fa sho. After taking the boys to school, he'd spin past her crib so she could polish his gun. But in the meantime, he was in bed with wifey who didn't even make him brick anymore.... She wouldn't even wear thongs; she wore briefs. He couldn't understand why she had become so boring. There was no chemistry between them anymore. Petie reached over and put his hand on her thigh. "Petie, I'm not in the mood," she said. She kissed him on the cheek and rolled over. "Goodnight," she added.

"Goodnight, ma. I love you," Petie replied.

"Yeah, I love you, too."

Petie lay there for a few moments and cut off the TV. No problem; he could go to bed brick tonight. He wasn't in the mood for her anyway. No sweat off his back. He would go see Des in the morning and then go and check Alexis. He had it all planned. *Yeah, I need my sleep anyway,* he thought looking over at Renee.

Chapter Three

Share rubbed baby oil on her legs after taking a hot shower. She hated when Petie had to go; she wanted them to wake up and cook breakfast, kick back and watch the morning news together.

She couldn't wait until Renee went to Pennsylvania to see her mother; every month she'd go for a weekend to spend time with her. Petie would then take his sons to their aunt's house, and that would be he and Share's weekend together. Renee had already visited her mother this month, so Share knew that weekends with Petie were out until next month. No problem; Petie would be back the night after tomorrow. He always came through every other night.

Share wasn't sure if she loved Petie, but she knew her feelings were stronger for him than the others. However, she knew she could have any man she wanted. She looked good, was self employed, had her own dough and no kids. She only needed a man for sexual pleasures.

When her father passed away she was the only benefactor on his insurance. She took that money and invested it, and with the profit she invested more. After two years of saving, she bought a brownstone and rented it out. All three floors were rented within two months. She only rented to Africans because she knew they worked two and three jobs and their rent would always be on time. She didn't want to have to be dragging anybody to court. Her tenants were hard workers, trying to make better lives for themselves. And she didn't have to worry about any drugs being on her property because she chose her tenants wisely; she ran background and credit checks before she even thought about leasing any of her apartments.

Share owned four brownstones altogether, and she lived in one of them. She was also the owner of two McDonald's restaurants, which were doing very well in sales, as well as a getaway co-op on Seventy-Fourth Street and West End Avenue. She was paid.

Share examined herself in her full length mirror. "Gotta start doing crunches again, girl," she said out loud. Share had a nice shape; she was thick with round hips, a small waistline, nice breasts and no stretch marks. She kept her hair at shoulder length, even though it could grow almost to the middle of her back. She wasn't impressed with hair; the longer it was the more work she had to put in it, she felt. Share wasn't like her mother, whose hair was almost down to her butt. She hadn't cut it in over ten years. She was definitely a hair freak.

Share unwrapped her doobie and went into the den to do

some work on her computer. She checked her e-mail and saw that Venus had sent her two messages, notifying her that all of her money transfers went through fine and that she would see her tomorrow for dinner. She made a mental note to call Venus to see where they would be dining and what they were going to wear. Until then it was time to get some sleep. She was tired and would have a long day tomorrow.

Will was pissed at Share; he hadn't seen her in over a week and he was hungry. She was like food to him. He actually had a crush on her before becoming manager of her McDonald's on 125th Street and Fordham Road. He had just come home from Upstate and was on *shock* parole. Those parole officers didn't play. He had to find a job quick or they would violate him. He had just barely graduated from the Shock Program, so when his P.O. said, "Get a job and find one quick," he did. He went to the McDonald's on 125th and was hired on the spot. He was grateful.

Will mopped floors and wiped tables before finally being trained to work the grill. Share would come through and look over the books, and she would tell Abdul, the manager, what needed to be changed and what could stay the same. He thought that she was probably a district manager. Whatever she was, Will thought she was definitely a chocolate cutie—about thirty-two, thirty-three, somewhere around there. She didn't wear a wedding ring and she always made extended eye contact with him. It didn't make a difference to him that he was only twenty-two; if she kept giving him that look, she could get it.

The idea of being with a woman in her thirties made Will's

gun jump. He was experienced with females, and he had chicks in all flavors—mostly young girls around seventeen or eighteen. One was sixteen, a Dominican chick. But he had never been with an older woman. His older brother was twenty-five, and his girl was thirty-six. He said older women were more mature and established, and they liked younger men. *That's all good. Maybe I'll start looking for an older shorty,* Will had begun to think.

It was closing time, and Will was mopping the back area. "Make sure the grills are turned off; Miss Jacobs is here," he heard Abdul say. Share came through and spoke to everyone. She walked past Will and touched his shoulder from behind. She said, "Excuse me. I'm sorry to walk on your floor, but I gotta get to the office."

"No problem, ma'am," Will replied.

"Call me Share; I'm only thirty-three, so I'm too young to be called *ma'am,*" Share said giving him a seductive smile.

"Oh, no doubt. I'll call you whatever you want me to," Will said turning slightly, looking at her out of the corner of his eye now. Share knew what time it was. She walked to Abdul's office as Will finished mopping the floor. He dropped the mop in the bucket and put everything else in its place. He wanted to be ready to leave when Share left. He threw on his hoodie and doo-rag and waited for Abdul to unlock his office door. After ending her meeting with him, Share stepped out the front door of the restaurant with Will right behind her. "Getting kind of chilly out here, huh? Winter is definitely coming," he said.

"Yeah, that's what it feels like. Where do you live?" Share said zipping up her jacket. The question threw Will off; he wasn't

expecting that so soon. He was about to lay his mack down, and here she was laying down hers.

"Who? Me? Oh yeah, of course me. I'm sorry; my bad. I live on Convent at 134th Street." Share started walking away, and Will didn't know if he should follow her. "Come on, dick, I'll give you a ride," she finally said. *Dick...oh, she mad ghetto,* he thought.

They talked all the way to Will's house, and he was surprised to find out that she owned the McDonald's and had property. He remembered his brother saying that older women were more mature, established and liked younger men. Share definitely fit that description. Will talked about his parole and how he was just beginning to adjust to being home and in the world again. She asked him personal questions about his life, if he had kids or a girlfriend, who he lived with and what he got arrested for. Will was honest about everything, except when she asked him about a shorty. "Nah, I'm not feeling nobody right now," he lied. "I've been home for like three weeks, and most of these young chicks are immature. I'm just staying solo for now." He could tell by the way she smiled that she liked the answer.

Will and Share sat in front of his building and talked some more until she had to go. He thanked her and got out, closing the door gently. In his eyes she had it all, plus she was thick with bedroom eyes.

About a week later Share asked Will if he knew how to paint; she needed her bathroom done. She told him she would pay him for the job in cash, and not to worry about his shift at McDonald's; she'd call Abdul and let him know he wouldn't be in. Will agreed to come and do her bathroom, and he thought about doing *her* in the bedroom—if she was with it.

Share's place was hot, like something out of a magazine. She showed Will the bathroom, supplied the paint, paid him $750.00 and went to the den to get some paperwork done.

Share was scheming. She liked this little boy. That was how she referred to all the young cats. She was actually in the den looking over Will's application. She knew he lived with his mother and that his salary wasn't much. But he looked like a young Petie—chocolate and muscle bound. The only difference was that Will was bow-legged. And so what if he was only twenty-two; he was experienced. Share was sure of that. Venus had told her about this young cat she used to deal with. Yeah, they knew what to do behind closed doors, even though some of them were possessive and could go into flip mode. Share didn't think Will would ever get like that...she would soon find out.

Will finished in the bathroom and walked into the den. He had taken off his shirt and was now showing off a nicely cut upper body along with a six-pack. Share turned away so he wouldn't see her blush. She thanked him and called him a cab. They were in bed together by that weekend. And just a few months later, he was managing the Fordham Road restaurant along with Abdul, and he was living in one of her brownstones on 146th and Riverside.

Will was now tight with Share because when he had called her earlier, some cat answered her phone and said she was busy. When he called back the phone just kept ringing—no answering machine, no nothing. He decided to call her again before sliding over. He didn't want to just pop up on her, not knowing what was what.

He wanted to know who this cat was answering her phone. Since he and Share had started their affair, he'd been faithful to her. He had cut off all the young girls. They couldn't be compared to Share; they couldn't even stand *next* to her as far as he was concerned. Now she had some nigga answering her phone. This was total disrespect. *She trying to play the kid,* Will thought. *Nah, won't be none of that.* He finally called her again, and after the fourth ring she answered. She told him she was lying down. "Who answered your phone when I hollered at you earlier?" Will asked her.

"Oh, that was nobody. My ex came by to get some of his things. Why didn't you call back?" she asked. Then she remembered Petie unhooking the phone, and she realized that if he *had* called back, she wouldn't have heard the phone ringing anyway.

"I did call back, but nobody picked up," Will said with attitude.

"Oh, you must have called when I walked him downstairs to let him out. That's probably what happened. Anyway, what's good? I'm hungry, ma. I wanna come and eat," Will said, already feeling himself swelling up.

Share thought about it for a minute. "Well, get here then," she said.

"I'm leaving now," Will said grabbing his coat. He snatched his keys off the hook, went outside and caught a cab. Share only lived on 142nd Street between Convent and Amsterdam. He could walk there, but he wanted to get there as soon as he could, and he called her on his cell to let her know he'd be outside in two minutes. He hurriedly paid the driver after the cab pulled up in front of Share's brownstone and waited for her to come downstairs.

Share was happy to see Will; he could finish where Petie left off. Petie never liked to do it in the kitty cat; he always wanted that booty shot. Either way she still had an orgasm, but she didn't just want it in the ass. And Will was only rough when she asked him to be. He took his time and did it the way she wanted him to. Will would put her to sleep easy and wake up in the middle of the night to go another round. He would massage her back and her feet, and when she woke up in the morning he would have French toast with turkey bacon waiting for her. He was so sweet, and she now wondered if he had another side that she just hadn't seen yet. She knew those young cats could spazz out quick, according to Venus, but she never gave him reason to.

Will's eyes began to dart about when they got upstairs, to see if anything appeared out of place. He was looking to see if any man's stuff was lying around that wasn't there before. He knew that some cat had been there, and now he wanted to know who it was. "So, your ex took all of his stuff out of here, huh?" he asked.

"Yeah, I called him and told him to come get his shit before I threw it out," Share lied.

"So he ain't got no reason to come back through here then, right?" It was more of a statement than a question.

"No, Will. He will not be coming through anymore. All right, honey?" Share said, hoping that would end the conversation. "Did you eat, baby?"

"Yeah, I went to my mom's house and had some roast beef, rice and spinach," Will replied. Share told him to get undressed and

come lay down. He missed her, and it seemed as if he hadn't seen her in months. He wanted to get inside of her. He felt at home when he was inside Share, and everything felt so right when he was with her. They were a perfect fit.

He lay down and cuddled up next to her. He gently rubbed her neck and turned her over onto her stomach. He went to the dresser, got the baby oil and dripped some down her back. He gently started massaging the oil into her back and over her butt cheeks. He squeezed her cheeks and spread them, running his fingers down the center of her ass. Will liked Share's ass. He wondered if one day she'd let him slide in there. He didn't think she was a freak like that, but one day he might just sniff her and catch her by surprise. However, tonight he just wanted to make love to her.

He turned her over onto her back and entered her slowly, savoring the feeling; she fit perfectly around him. She lightly moaned and wrapped her legs around his back as they moved in rhythm with one another. Will always made love to Share; those young chicks, he boned them. Plus he thought that some of them had a foul smell down there. Share always smelled fresh, and it seemed like she got tighter and tighter each time they were together. He stroked her until she begged him to stop. He could do that easily, and he could keep himself from busting off for as long as he wanted. No matter how tightly Share's muscles gripped him, he knew how to hold out.

Share was biting his chest and had her nails in his back. Will was hungry, and he wasn't giving her any mercy. He placed his hands underneath her and spread her cheeks while moving in and out of her. He arched his back, thrusting his full self inside her. *Nah, she gets no mercy,* he thought. He ran his hands through her hair and kissed her passionately until he could feel her begin to orgasm. He could no longer hold back now. He put her legs over his shoulders and went as deep as he could until he finally exploded. They lay there for a few minutes to catch their breath and then kissed.

"How you feel, ma?" Will asked.

"Like I need a cigarette," Share said, still a little out of breath. She really was thinking about smoking a cigarette, but she didn't want to give in to the temptation. She had been nicotine free for almost a month and she wanted to keep up her efforts.

Share used up a lot of her energy with Will, but she didn't mind because he always made her feel good. She got up, went to the bathroom and took a quick shower. When she came back to bed, Will was on the phone talking to one of the employees at the Fordham restaurant. He was a good manager, and she never worried about anything. Abdul had trained him well at the 125th Street location. He always checked on things, even on his day off. She liked the fact that he was not only a good lover, but he was responsible.

She leaned across his chest and started biting his chin and sucking on his bottom lip. He grabbed a handful of her hair and threw his tongue down her throat. They kissed until he pulled away and asked her, "You gonna feed me again or what, ma?" Share fell onto her back and propped herself up with a pillow.

"I can't take another round. Let's wait until morning," she said. She reached over and turned off the lamp, kissing Will one last time. "Goodnight, baby. Sleep with the angels."

if it ain't one thing
it's another

Chapter Four

Venus parked the car, grabbed her briefcase from off the back seat and walked down the steps. She lived on the ground floor of Share's brownstone on 144th right off Willis Avenue in the Bronx. As soon as she put the key in the door, Bullet began barking and jumping all over the place. He had gotten so big and strong that she had to push her way in every day. That was a good thing because Venus knew he held the house down while she was at work. And she never worried about anybody breaking into her place; Bullet would tear a mutha-fucka apart, so she definitely didn't need an alarm system. He didn't even want to let her man, BJ, in sometimes, let alone a stranger, and on days like today when the weather was good, Venus didn't think twice about leaving the front door open and allowing the late September breeze to flow through the screen door.

Bullet was jealous, like most male dogs with female owners, and Venus knew her dog was funny style. He was one of those sometimey dogs; some days he would bark and growl and some days he wouldn't. Venus loved that dog to death, and she couldn't wait until Diamond had their puppies.

Venus stepped into the living room and turned on the ceiling lights. She walked to the back to let Bullet out in the yard for a little while so he could do his thing. She then called Porscha, who rented a one-bedroom upstairs on the third floor, to let her know she was home and to come down a little later. Porscha told Venus that she was sending Diamond down so she and Bullet could spend time with each other. "Spend time with each other? That's why she's having puppies now," Venus said laughing. They talked about their pits like they were real people, and as far as they both were concerned, their dogs were smarter than a lot of people they knew.

Venus let Bullet inside and walked back to the front of the brownstone. He was fast on her heels now. "Oh, boy, be quiet; she's coming." Bullet seemed to know when Diamond was coming down. He was patiently waiting by the time Porscha let Diamond downstairs. Diamond was his pit chick. Bullet barked and ran behind her to smell her butt. She lifted up her tail and then went into the living room and spread out on the carpet. Bullet followed and lay beside her, licking her nipples. She was going to have those puppies any day now. Venus watched Bullet licking Diamond's nipples until he gave her a 'beat it' look. *Yeah, my dog is definitely human,* she thought.

Venus checked her messages to see if Share had received

the e-mail she sent her. She hadn't. She had tried calling her, but the phone just kept ringing. She knew Petie was there and that Share probably had a dick in her ass and couldn't get to the phone.

Venus went into her bedroom, got undressed and put on a pair of shorts and sneakers. She popped her aerobic videotape into the DVR for her daily workout and did a couple of stretches before the music started. She set the timer on her watch and began her usual thirty-minute exercise routine. She went to the kitchen when she was done and got a big glass of ice water. As she sat at the kitchen table catching her breath, Diamond started growling and Bullet jumped up and raced to the front window. Venus heard a car door close outside and then her gate being opened. She knew it was BJ when she heard his keys. Diamond and Bullet were both growling now, just waiting for the door to open. Bullet was bearing down on his front legs in an assault position and Diamond was to his right, holding him down. Venus looked on from the kitchen, observing how well the two pits were guarding the house.

BJ had stopped at Pathmark on 125th Street to pick up some milk, juice, Applejacks for him and Fruity Pebbles for Venus. He also picked up a twenty-pound bag of Pedigree for Bullet, and he had copped some trees from his man, Derek, outside a corner bodega, where he purchased a Heineken and a pack of cigarettes. They talked for a few minutes, and BJ told him that Diamond would be having her pups any day now. BJ knew Derek wanted one, so he told him that he would sell him a newborn baby pit for a hundred— take it or leave it. Derek agreed to it, but he was hoping that BJ would just give him one on GP. Derek told BJ that he would throw

him a buck next time he came through on the strength that he gave him first dibs on the puppies. BJ agreed. He knew that Venus and Porscha each wanted to keep one for themselves. The rest they would sell.

When BJ had slammed the car door, he saw Bullet jumping up and down in the front window. If it hadn't been closed, he would have jumped right through it. Now here he was, trying to get inside the house with grocery bags and his backpack.

BJ pushed the door open, stepped around the dogs and went straight to the kitchen where he put everything away. Then he hung his coat up in the closet and pulled out a phillie and a dime bag to roll. "Ma, what's good," he yelled out when he heard the shower running.

"Ain't nothin'. Come wash my back," Venus yelled back. She had always attracted younger guys, and it seemed like they understood her better than men her own age.

BJ walked into the bathroom with his Sean John's hanging off his ass and a doo-rag tightly secured around his braids. *This nigga looks so good,* Venus thought to herself. Even after almost a year, she was still infatuated with him.

BJ took a bar of soap and lathered up the scrubbie that Venus handed him. She tilted her head back, letting the water from the showerhead beat down on her scalp. He ran the soap from her chin down to her nipples, circling them with the edge of the soap until they were hard as peanut brittle. "Turn around, ma," he said, "and put your hands on the wall."

Venus loved being in this position with BJ, when she played

the cop and he played the robber. "Like this, baby?" she asked in her sultriest voice. She arched her back and stood on her tiptoes while demonstrating the pat-and-search position.

"Yeah, ma, just like that. Don't move," BJ said. He had jumped out of his Timbs and jeans and was now stepping out of his boxers. He slid off his socks and T-shirt and was up in Venus with one swift movement. He held her hands against the wall as she bent forward and gave her the anaconda. Water was all over the floor now, and their bodies were slippery with lather when BJ let loose. His body shook and his legs became weak. He stood under the showerhead and washed the sweat from his body. Then he dried himself off and went to roll up his vanilla flavored blunt.

Porscha called downstairs and BJ told her that Venus was in the shower. He told her she'd call her back when she got out, but Porscha didn't wait. She called her sponsor and went to a Narcotics Anonymous meeting on 139th and St. Ann's; she had to make a meeting every day. *No matter what happens, don't use,* she'd always keep in mind. Porscha had been doing all right since she came home, but lately she felt like getting high. However, she was scared to use and she was afraid of failing and losing everything she had worked so hard for; so she made her meetings and stayed connected.

When she got back home she noticed that Venus' living room lights were out, so she went right upstairs. Venus had left her a message, saying that she was crashing for the night and would call her in the morning.

Porscha got undressed and laid back to read her basic text:

Recovery and Relapse and How It Works. She had just celebrated two years of being clean. *No matter what, don't pick up,* she thought.

Chapter Five

Petie had two bowls of Cap'n Crunch and some orange juice and bagels for his little men. Renee was getting them dressed and putting their books in their book bags. They wore doo-rags that matched their outfits, and today they'd each wear one of their many North Face jackets. They had one in every color, so they were crisp every day.

"Dad, what we havin'?" Darnell asked Petie. Darnell was his first born and stubborn just like he was.

"Cap'n Crunch without the berries, bagels and some orange juice," Petie answered.

"Dad, I don't want Cap'n Crunch this morning; gimme some Frosted Flakes and let Dante have the Cap'n Crunch."

"Listen, little man, eat what Daddy fixed for you and tomor-

row I'll remember to fix you frosties, aiight?" Petie said, waiting for him to protest.

"Good morning, Dad. What's good?" Dante said reaching for the milk and cereal. Dante was the slow one; he never did anything on time. He was more like Renee; he took his time with everything.

"You, little man, that's what's good," Petie said smiling at him. He always let his sons know that it was about them, that they were somebody important and special. It was definitely working, because they were both conceited already. He knew they were going to be a piece of work when they hit their teens.

Petie dropped them off at school and called Alexis. He told her that he was coming through today and to go and pick up a box of umbrellas. He then call Des and told her to listen for the bell; he would be there any minute. She was with it, and she liked talking on his microphone...a one-two, a one-two.... She was a dick jockey fa sho.

Petie parked the truck and rang Des's bell. She buzzed him right in, and her door was already open when he stepped out of the elevator.

Her place always smelled like a litter box. She had two cats, and they always wanted to rub on his legs. Petie hated those cats, and their hair was all over the place. He never looked, but he was sure there was cat hair in her refrigerator. That's why he never wanted anything to drink. It was more like, "Come drink me so I can get outta here."

Des was losing weight. Petie wondered if she was smoking

31

on the down low; her hands were looking darker than the rest of her body and she was always in the bathroom, which was the case now. Yeah, she was hitting the stem. He sold enough drugs to know the signs when he saw them.

"Come on, let's go," Des said coming back into the living room where Petie was sitting on the couch. "I got something to do after you leave."

Yeah, go cop, Petie thought. He opened up his jeans and pulled his gun through the zipper hole; he didn't want to take off his jeans and get cat hair all over them. She kneeled down in front of him and ran her tongue along the sides of his dick. She opened her jaws and deep throated him. He thought she was going to choke. He placed his hands on the crown of her head to help her along. "Yeah, that's what I'm talkin' 'bout, ma...yeah, like that. Keep your chin up, Des...yeah, a little more...don't stop," Petie said coaching her along. Damn, she was good. She could suck the skin off a beef stick.

Petie didn't bother to hold back. He busted off, and she held his cum in her mouth and ran to the bathroom to spit it out. When she came out, Petie went in, washed himself off and told her he would call her tomorrow morning. Before leaving he gave her three dime bags of crills and a ten-dollar bill.

"Nigga, what's this? I don't smoke," Des said trying to play it off.

"Sho' you right. Take it and sell it then," Petie said before walking out and slamming the door. He was done with her. He never fucked with chicks who smoked that shit. He decided to find a new

head nurse. He could easily replace her. *I'm that nigga,* he said to himself.

Petie called Ladelle to let him know he was on his way to pick him up. They had to go to Mitchell projects to pick up their money and throw the workers some more material. Petie threw on *Tupac's Greatest Hits* CD and headed to the Polo Grounds to pick up his partner.

Renee slid on a red thong with a valentine heart in the center. She put on the matching bra and rubbed some Ocean Dream over her skin. She loved the way the Muslim Oil smelled, and so did her lover. She called him and was disappointed to hear that he had to make a run and would see her in about an hour. She put on a porno DVD and laid back and masturbated. That would hold her until she saw him. She enjoyed dropping down and getting her eagle on for him. He took his time and made her feel wanted. Petie just did the damn thing and that was it. He did it like he was punishing her or some-thing. She didn't even like him touching her anymore.

Even after two kids, Renee still looked good—no stretch marks or fat pockets. And she felt good about herself, too. She just didn't have it for Petie anymore. The only thing holding them togeth-er was Darnell and Dante; if it weren't for them she would have been gone. But that didn't stop Renee from doing her. She saw her lover five days a week, and she was sexually satisfied. She fixed herself a cup of coffee and raisin bread with jelly, and waited for him to call.

Chapter
Six

Will went to the kitchen and started making breakfast. Some time during the middle of the night he woke up, and Share had him in her mouth. Afterward she got on top of him and rode him like a chick on a motorcycle with no helmet. He firmly grabbed her butt, spreading her cheeks. They came at the same time and Share fell back to sleep on his chest. Will knew he had a sleepy dick; he put chicks to sleep after just one round.

Will made grits with cheddar cheese and onions. He knew what Share liked to eat. He had made it his business to learn her, and that's exactly what he did. She was his princess. He knew her eating habits, how she slept, her facial expressions, what kind of books she liked to read and the type of movies she liked to watch. He knew almost everything about her. She was the only thing that

mattered to him, beside his mother, and he was certain that God had brought them together.

Will woke Share and they ate breakfast and watched the news. She complimented him on the good breakfast and asked him to make a deposit for her this morning. She didn't feel like going out this afternoon, but she wanted the money to be in her account. She told him she opened up a new one at the bank on 145th Street and St. Nicholas, and to take the car and drive over there for her. Share gave him a deposit slip and nine grand in an envelope. She trusted Will; he had proved himself trustworthy. Will grabbed the envelope and the car keys, slipped on his jeans and hoodie and headed out the door.

Petie and Ladelle had finished their business in Mitchell projects and were coming back over the bridge. The money was right...those cats never came up short. If they did, Petie would send a Harlem team over there six cars deep and niggas would be thrown from rooftops.

Ladelle was a no-nonsense nigga, too. He and Petie grew up together, got money together and regulated together. He was Petie's mi-dan.

They were driving up the 145th Street hill, approaching St. Nicholas. Petie pulled the truck up to the side of the train station and peered through his rearview mirror. After about fifteen minutes, he saw a young cat leave the bank and get in Share's car. He told Ladelle what he had just seen.

"Follow that nigga," Ladelle said, and Petie trailed him all the way to Share's brownstone. Will got out of the car and hit the alarm.

He walked up Share's front steps and stuck the key in the door.

"Oh, shit. She gave some little boy the keys to her crib, La. Who she think she playin' wit, dick? I should go ring the bell and put her on front street," Petie said. He was vexed. He couldn't believe what he had just seen. *Maybe it was her nephew,* he thought. *Nah, that ain't no nephew.*

"Yo, pull off, nigga. Let's ride. Fuck that ho," Ladelle said. He didn't want Petie to dwell on it too much, because he knew that at any minute he'd be banging on her door. He would snatch her out of the house and stomp her like a Newport. Ladelle wasn't ready for this type of drama at ten in the morning. "Come on, my nigga. Let's roll. See her later," Ladelle pressed. They pulled off and drove back to the Polo Grounds. Petie dropped Ladelle off and headed for Alexis' house.

chapter seven

Renee was washing her coffee mug out when the phone rang. It was him. He told her to get a cab to the hotel and he'd be outside. She grabbed a box of condoms and dabbed some Muslin oil between her thighs and called a cab. She met him at the hotel on St. Nicholas between 152nd and 153rd Streets. They got a room and headed upstairs.

Renee pulled off her clothes and unbuckled her lover's belt. He was already hard. They kissed and he went down south, sucking and licking until she exploded. Then she returned the favor until she couldn't wait any longer. She assumed the doggy style position, and he grabbed her cheeks and entered her, moving like a professional. "Do Petie make you sing like I do?" he asked.

"No, he could never do it like you, baby pa," Renee replied.

They went on and on until he came. His body shuddered and he gripped her butt even harder now. Finally he pulled out of her and lay back on the bed. He grabbed the TV remote and watched ESPN as they talked about the kids, money, crime and politics. Renee liked the fact that he was an intellect. No matter what they discussed, he always had something worthwhile to contribute to the topic.

They ordered Chinese food and went at it again. Five hours later it was time to go, even though there were many more hours available on the room. Renee knew Petie would be home with the boys and she wanted to be there. They kissed and left the hotel separately. She called a cab and went home to find the house empty. *Oh, well,* she thought—*shower time.*

Petie was on his way to pick up Darnell and Dante after leaving Alexis' house. He was so angry at Share that he dug Alexis a new hole. He couldn't wait to get at Share. "She'd better have a good explanation as to why that young buck was pushing her Lexus and had the keys to her crib—not to mention coming out the bank. I know she ain't got son handling her money. Yo, she gon' make me hurt her," he said out loud to himself.

When Petie and the boys got home Renee wasn't there, so they dropped off their book bags and headed to the park. Petie watched them play football with some other kids their age as he made calls to the Bronx to check on his money. He hollered at Ladelle and told him to bag up 150 more dimes so they could drop them off in the morning. Ladelle told him to come through as soon as he took his sons to school. He'd be waiting.

The dogs barking awakened Venus and BJ from a good sleep. She looked over at the clock; she knew by the time that Bullet and Diamond were barking at the African guy on his way to work. She rolled over and went back to sleep. BJ moved up behind her and wrapped his legs around hers. She knew he'd be getting up soon for work, so she let him sleep. He needed his rest. She decided to get up and prepare some home fries and eggs with toast for him before he went off to work.

Share was still in bed when Will got back. He took a shower, got dressed and woke her up to let her know he was leaving again. "Take the keys. I'll see you tonight," Share said.

"No doubt, ma. I'm closing up, so I'll be back here about eleven-thirty," Will replied.

"Okay, baby. And stop somewhere and get a set of keys made for you. The ones you have are the ones I always let Venus hold."

"Aiight, I'll see you tonight," Will said before bending down to kiss her. He took her car keys off the ring, placed them on the night table and locked the door behind him. He walked to Amsterdam and caught a cab to Fordham Road.

Venus and BJ ate breakfast and made love, and he went off to work feeling happy as ever. *Damn, ain't nothing like an older chick*, he thought. He got in the car and drove to Lincoln Hospital where he did custodial maintenance. The job paid almost eleven an hour. He liked that legal money, and his family was proud of him. Venus always encouraged him to strive for the best.

He hollered at his man on his lunch break to see what was up for the weekend. Will couldn't talk too long because three people had called in sick and he had to work the grill. He told BJ he would see him Saturday night for sure.

BJ and Will had gone to school together. It was BJ who had told Will to check the McDonald's on 125th Street, because he knew they would hire him. He didn't mention that the owner was his girl's best friend. BJ had already called Abdul and told him that he was sending a friend over, and asked him if he could hire him on his strength. Abdul knew BJ was living with Venus, and that she was Share's best friend. He didn't want to upset anybody, so he hired Will the day he came in and filled out the application.

When Will started seeing Share, BJ finally told him that Share was his girl's best friend. "Oh, word? You serious, dog?" Will had said, thinking how small New York really is.

"On the strength," BJ replied. BJ went on to tell him about the call he'd made to Abdul, because he knew Abdul only liked to hire foreigners. He also told Will about him and Venus, and how she had just about moved him right into her place.

Petie parked the truck and went inside the house with the boys. Renee was cooking dinner when they came in, and she asked them where they had been and how was school. Petie came up behind her and kissed the back of her neck.

"Petie, please, I'm cooking," Renee said.

"Why every time I touch you it's always 'Petie this and Petie that'?" he asked. He now had his suspicions.

"Because you always catching me when I'm not in the mood. And when I am in the mood, you're not around," Renee answered, pissed at herself for explaining anything to him. Shit, he never explained anything to her. Petie gave her a 'whatever' look before going into the bedroom and lying down.

He was gonna creep by Share's crib and catch her out

there. He wanted to be sure before he broke her jaw, even though his gut told him that he was absolutely right.

Darnell and Dante told Petie and Renee about their day as they all ate dinner. They talked about how they had chased the girls around the school playground. Dante told them about Yolanda, the little girl who kissed him. "Yuck," he said. Darnell began to laugh. Yolanda liked Dante. She sat next to him in class, and she would always try to help him with his math.

"I would have told her, 'Let me see something, and then I'll let you kiss me.' Right, Dad?" he said smiling at Petie. *Ah, man,* Petie thought. *He blowin' up my spot.* Renee cut her eyes at him. He would have to talk to the boys a little later about keeping their conversations a secret, mainly because of her. He was molding his little men to be playas—not the ones to get played.

Venus showered, got dressed in a Donna Karan suit and headed to work. She was a supervisor at Chase Manhattan on 168th Street and Broadway. She handled the accounts and money transfers. Share kept an account there, so Venus always checked on it and did any money transfers when necessary. She and Share were having dinner tonight, and later she'd go over to Share's and cook some baby back ribs, macaroni and cheese and collard greens.

Andre walked up to Venus and handed her a cup of coffee with vanilla creamer. She thanked him and watched him walk away. Andre was a cutie, but he was her age, which meant he was too old. And besides, she only had it for BJ.

Venus knew Andre liked her. A couple of times they went to lunch together and had a drink after work, but that was all. She wouldn't cheat on BJ; she wasn't loose like that anymore, so she ignored him and didn't play into his seductive glances.

Share was at the 125th Street restaurant, discussing the new menus that would start next month. She talked to the new employees and let them know what she expected from them and what she wouldn't tolerate. She had a good crew at the 125th Street restaurant, and she owed it all to Abdul for choosing them carefully. As a matter of fact, there was always a good crew there, and Share trusted his judgment. Abdul was very efficient and professional when it came to business.

Will, on the other hand, hired ex-cons. He considered it giving back; someone gave him a chance, and now he was giving others coming home a chance. Share liked that Will hadn't forgotten where he came from. He was faithful and consistent, which was why she finally gave him a set of keys. She was tired of Petie and his back-breaker calls. Besides, Petie never made love to her; he only boned her. She was done with him; enough was enough. Share made a mental note to holla at him and let him know to lose her number. Even though Will was eleven years younger than her, she had decided to settle down with him. Venus and BJ were doing fine, so why couldn't she and Will do the same? *Yeah, I'm gonna cut that nigga off tonight,* she thought as she got in her car.

Renee washed the dishes and put them away. Petie was playing Play Station with the boys, and she knew as soon as it got dark he would be hitting the streets. That was his M.O. it didn't matter to her because he paid the bills and kept their sons in the latest gear. And she knew he wouldn't be around long because parole was looking for him. He hadn't reported in four weeks, so his P.O dropped a warrant on him. They had come to the house a couple of times, but Petie wasn't there—lucky him. Renee remembered the last time they violated him. They hit him with ninety days and she spent all her free time with her lover. But Petie made sure that money was left for the rent, phone and cable bill. The one thing she gave him credit for was being responsible. He never let her or her kids be without the things they needed and wanted.

She went into the boys' bedroom, picked out their outfits for the next day and ironed them. Then she ran a bath for Dante first, since he was the slow one.

After bathing, the boys watched the Nickelodeon channel with Renee. Petie had changed his clothes and was preparing to go out. *Bye*, Rene thought. She would be asleep by the time he came back.

Her lover would be calling in the morning for their usual session. She met him every morning except on Saturdays and Sundays, mainly because the kids were home then. But Monday through Friday, it was on and poppin'.

Chapter Nine

Petie jumped in the truck and called Share on her cell phone. "Yo, who was driving your car this morning?" he demanded before even saying hello.

"Listen, don't worry about who was driving my car, nigga. Last time I checked, *I* paid for it and the title was in *my* name," Share barked.

"Oh, you got a lot of mouth over the phone, gangsta. I'ma see you in a little while—ya heard?"

"No, no, I don't think that's possible. Look, I'm busy and I'm not in the mood for you tonight or any other night, so lose my number, Petie. It was fun while it lasted, but my plate is full," Share said preparing to hang up.

"Yo, who the fuck you think you talkin' to—some twenty-cent nigga? Bitch, you don't tell me no dumb shit like—" *Click*. Share had already hung up. Petie could not believe this chick. He called her right back.

"What?!" Share said with attitude.

"Yo, stop talking to me like I'm one of your burger flippers. You don't run this shit—I do. Don't make me come over there...." *Click*. Petie couldn't believe this shit. He started to think that maybe she was on mental meds or something; there was no way she was talking to him like that in her right mind.... He now knew that his suspicions were right from the beginning; it was that young cat. Petie decided to wait until she got home and then bring the drama. He wasn't gonna do that at her restaurant and disrespect her like that. But he would definitely catch her at the crib, smack her around, pull her hair and run up in her ass for talking mad shit. "Yeah, I got something for you, ma," he said grinning from ear to ear.

Share parked her car and called Venus at the bank. She needed to vent. After being put on hold for a few minutes, Venus came on the line. "This is Venus Winters, how can I help you?" she said not knowing that it was Share on the other end.

"Girl, you are not gonna believe what just happened," Share said. She told Venus about the phone call from Petie, and how she told him not to call her anymore.

Venus could tell that Share was shaken up by the tone of her voice. "Share, you knew he was wild-style when you started fuckin' him, so what made you think he wouldn't flip on you too? You better get a restraining order and let Will know so he can be on point," Venus said starting to worry. She knew Petie would bring the

drama—right to Share's door.

They talked about their dinner date for tonight and Venus said she would stop at the meat store to get what she needed to cook. They agreed to meet at Share's place at five-thirty. Venus wanted to be home by the time BJ came. He had a class tonight and she knew he'd be home around nine, plus she had to feed Bullet.

Share hung up and leaned back in the driver's seat, thinking about whether to tell Will about Petie. She didn't want to, but Venus was right. She had to so he could be on point. Petie was possessive and she didn't know what length he would go to in order to prove his point. She decided to let Will know soon. Besides, she figured it would give them a fresh start, with no lies or secrets.

Porscha was about to leave work and go to a meeting. She worked at the same rehab center where she had once been a resident. After serving eight months for possession, she came home and went into a twenty-eight-day program. After graduating from the program, she maintained her sobriety, stayed in touch with the staff and later joined them as a counselor.

She was driving up 135th on her way to the Bronx when Giselle called her. Giselle was Porscha's wife. They had been together since she had left the program, and they were in love. Porscha told her that she was on her way home, and Giselle said she'd meet her there after stopping at the grocery store and getting something for them to eat.

Porscha would never go back to men. Giselle made her feel

good, and she made love to Porscha better than any man she'd ever been with. Porscha would cook a full course meal, and they would make love and lean back for the remainder of the evening. Porscha stepped on the gas, anxious to see Giselle and forgetting about her NA meeting.

Will was vexed after Share had told him about Petie, but he was neither impressed nor depressed about the nigga. He called his boys, BJ and Kalif, to let them know he might have some drama with a knucklehead. "Your beef is my beef, son," Kalif said.

"Let's set it on this cat...anytime you get ready," BJ said. Kalif and BJ were his left and right hands. Will was closer to them than he was with his own brother. They were always already to set it on whoever—ride or die.

Will wasn't having it. "Knucklehead callin' my girl poppin' shit. Nah, scrams, it won't be none of that," he said talking out loud to himself now. Share had told him where she was parked, and he told her to wait there; he'd get a cab from the restaurant and they could drive home together. She told him to tell Abdul that she'd said to close up.

Will counted up the money in the safe and put the total on the safe sheet. He called Share before leaving and told her he'd see her soon. He went out to the street and hailed a cab.

Petie called Share's number and got no answer. He figured she was-n't home yet, but he drove past her house to see if her car was there and she just wasn't picking up the phone. He drove around her block twice and decided to go back home. *Give her time to get in*, he thought.

Kalif was outside waiting for BJ when he got off from work. Kalif was packing heat and ready for whatever. They hopped in BJ's car and headed to Manhattan. BJ called Share and asked if Will was there yet. Share had told him that Will was on his way to meet her and she told him the exact spot where she was parked.

"Aiight, tell son we comin' across the bridge. Don't leave till we pull up." Then he called Venus to find out where she was. She was headed to the meat store to pick up a couple of pounds of baby back ribs and cheese for the baked macaroni. Kalif got on the phone and asked her if she knew Petie and what kind of car he drove. Venus told Kalif everything, and she stressed that he was wild-style.

"I don't give a fuck. Nigga ain't 'bout it like my team," Kalif said ready to set it. He was 'bout it for sho, and he had a hard body. The only things soft on him were his balls.

Kalif and BJ pulled up to the location Share had given them, and she and Will were already in the car waiting. BJ hopped out and hollered at Will for a minute and they decided to wait for Venus. BJ didn't want his girl coming alone in case this cat was waiting or some shit. He called Venus and she told him she was two blocks away from Share's house. BJ could hear the worry in her voice, so he pulled off to go meet her and Will followed him with Share now in the passenger seat of her car.

Venus turned onto Share's block preparing to park, and she couldn't believe what she saw. Petie's truck was parked across the street from Share's apartment. "Oh, shit," she said. She rode past the truck to make sure it was him—it was, and DMX's *Niggaz Done Started Something* was blasting from his system. Venus knew Petie wouldn't recognize her because she had bought a new car since he last saw her. She turned the corner, pulled out her cell phone and called BJ. Two cars behind her started honking their horns; she hadn't even noticed that the light had turned green. She pulled off to the side and told BJ what she had just seen.

"Oh, yeah, ma? Listen: park the car and wait outside the building. We about five minutes away. Will said he has your keys, so just wait on the steps and make sure the nigga sees you," BJ said anxious to get there.

Petie was in the truck talking to Alexis when he saw Venus approaching Share's house. He turned his music down and beckoned her over to him. She shook her head no and kept it moving.

"Oh, you don't know nobody no more, huh?" Petie yelled out to her from where he was parked across the street. Venus said nothing. She didn't even look his way. Petie got out of the truck and crossed the street.

BJ and Kalif turned onto Share's block and double-parked. Will and Share pulled up and parked behind them. He told Share to go into the house with Venus. Share got out of the car and pulled out her keys. "Let's go," she told Venus after walking right past Petie.

"Oh, you can't speak to daddy unless we in the bed, huh bitch?" Share put her key in the door and opened it, and she and

Venus went inside the brownstone. Petie ran up and stuck his foot in the doorway to prevent Share from closing the door back. "That's all right, Share; I really want to hit your friend anyway. Your asshole stinks," he said before moving his foot.

Petie never saw BJ, Kalif or Will double-parked up the block, and now he was so busy harassing Share that he didn't notice them pull up; he was far from on point. As he turned to leave, Will clipped him and said, "Hold that, old man." Petie reached inside his coat and Kalif pulled out on him. Petie froze. He wasn't used to niggas putting guns in his face; he put guns in nigga's faces.

Everything happened so quickly. Will began spitting out razors, and one caught Petie across his cheek. Another one hit him across the nose. He was leaking. Petie grabbed at him but couldn't focus with all the blood, and BJ kicked him in the cut on his cheek. When he fell, Kalif pistol whipped him while BJ and Will stomped him. Afterward they picked his bloody ass up and threw him in his truck.

"I should take this shit and let my man step it. What you think?" Kalif asked Will.

"Nah, we don't need nothing from this old man," Will replied.

"Fuck him and his truck," BJ said cutting in, "but not that ice on his neck and pinky finger—I'm baggin' him." Petie was out cold with blood coming out of his ear, dripping onto the seats. BJ took his keys out of the ignition and dropped them down a nearby sewer. They didn't know whether Petie was dead or not—and they didn't care. They headed up the steps of Share's brownstone like nothing happened. After getting comfortably inside, they rolled up two blunts.

Share and Venus had seen everything from the front window

of Share's apartment. It was their first time seeing the young men in action, and they had both watched with surprise.

"They gonna kill him," Share had said when she saw Kalif pull out the heat and point it at Petie's forehead.

"No they won't; they just givin' him a message," Venus replied.

Chapter Ten

Ladelle had been trying to call Petie for over an hour, and he was wondering if parole snatched him up. He could always reach Petie and couldn't understand why he wasn't answering his phone. He called Renee and Alexis to see if they'd heard from him. Renee said she hadn't, and Alexis told him she'd been waiting for him to come by since seven o' clock. It was now eight-thirty, and Ladelle was sure that parole had picked him up.

He decided to go and see Big Lou over on 140th and Amsterdam. Lou was on their team; maybe he had heard something.

Renee was calling Petie's phone every five minutes. She figured he was laid up with one of his playthings. But she didn't care; she had her own. She called Ladelle back and he told her that there was still no word from Petie. He didn't mention anything about Alexis waiting for him to come by and he never showed up. Ladelle thought he might be with Share, but he dismissed the idea because he knew she was a late night thing; it was only nine-fifteen, so he wouldn't be there now. Ladelle headed over to Big Lou's crib.

Share and her guests ordered take-out from Domino's Pizza. Cooking anything was out of the question now. Venus no longer had an apetite; she was deep in thought.

Share was worried; she was hoping that none of her neighbors had seen anything from their windows. She was worried that Petie might be dead. His truck was still on her block, so that meant he was either dead or out cold. She hoped he was out cold.

Kalif had made some phone calls and said that some of his peeps were going to come through and stay on the first floor for the night. Share didn't mind; there were three apartments down on the first floor, so it was no big deal to her. Besides, she only used the second and third floors. She considered telling Kalif that they could stay until the shit boiled over. Share was scared; she knew Petie's peeps and how they moved. There would be problems behind this. She knew it was about to get ugly.

Porscha had already called Venus twice and left two messages on her answering machine. Venus hadn't called her back yet. That was strange; she always called when she got home from work. It was after nine-thirty and BJ wasn't there either. Porscha called Venus' cell

phone and her voicemail came on. *What is going on?* Before going
into a panic, she called Share and was relieved to find that everyone
was there.

"Oh, y'all bitches had drama and nobody hollered at me?
What that be about?" Porscha said. Share explained to her that it
wasn't female drama—it was Petie. She told Porscha that if they had
chick drama she would have hollered at her immediately. She
assured her that she was okay and would call her tomorrow.

Porscha and Giselle finished their dinner and were drinking
Alize to wash it down when the phone rang. It was Lou and Ladelle.
They were calling to see if Giselle had heard from her uncle. Giselle
said that she had spoken to Petie yesterday, and she wondered if
parole picked him up. Giselle called Renee and asked her if she'd
heard from Petie.

"Probably laid up with some ho," Renee said nonchalantly.
Giselle hung up the phone and thought about the whole thing. She
remembered that parole was looking for Petie, and she was now certain that they had picked him up. She looked over at Porscha and
then started playing with her hair. Giselle loved her. Porscha had a
reddish, Indian complexion with straight hair, deep dimples and full
lips. Men always tried to holla at her, but Giselle had her on lock.
Porscha got up to undress, and then she walked into the bathroom
to turn on the shower. Giselle followed her.

Petie's head was throbbing, and it hurt when he breathed. The time on the dashboard read ten-twenty. He didn't know where he was and his vision was blurry. His body and head felt heavy. He reached for the handle on the door, opened it and fell out. He was fucked up. Petie got to his feet and staggered up the block towards Amsterdam Avenue. Musical lyrics rang out from his phone: I get high, high, high, high, hiiiigh...I get high, high, high, high, hiiiiiggh.... *What is that—the Smurfs?* he thought. *What is that noise? Oh, God, we're being invaded by blue people....* Petie's mind wasn't functioning properly, and he couldn't figure out the simple fact that his phone was ringing. It rang again, and this time different music played. Petie fell forward, and he was leaning against somebody's car now. He fumbled around in his pocket and pulled out his phone. He was still incoherent, but at least this time he knew to reach for his phone. He pushed the answer key. "Yo, dick, where the fuck you at?" he heard Ladelle say.

"Im...I'm...on da ground...beef, dick...come g-get me."

"You got beef, nigga? Where? Where you at, dick? Where the fuck you at?!" Ladelle screamed into the phone. Petie was like a brother to him. If he had beef, Ladelle was gonna empty out on somebody.

"Sh-a-a-a-re...Sh-a-a-a-re's house," Petie slurred.

"Don't move. Me and Lou is on our way," Ladelle said before running out with Lou on his heels. They took three steps at a time and jumped in the Hummer parked outside Lou's crib.

"Yo, the nigga said he at Share's house. Bitch on 142nd own them brownstones and shit," Ladelle said. He told Lou how fucked up Petie had sounded. They turned onto Share's block and didn't

see Petie but saw his truck. Ladelle parked, and he and Lou immediately got out of the Hummer and began searching up and down the
block for him. Finally they saw him slumped over a parked car.
Ladelle ran over to him and bent down to get a closer look at his
man. Petie's head was swollen and he had razor cuts on his face,
with old and new blood. Ladelle wasn't sure, but it looked like he had
lost some teeth. "Call a fucken ambulance!" he told Lou.

Petie screamed when they took off his jacket, and he winced
when they stood him straight up. There was blood coming out of his
ears and dripping from his wounds. Lou was getting teary-eyed now.
He, Petie and Ladelle had all grown up together. Petie and Ladelle
pushed bricks in the BX and Lou kept it uptown.... This shit couldn't
be happening. Somebody was gonna die behind this shit.

The ambulance arrived and Petie was put on a stretcher. His
pulse and blood pressure were low, and the EMTs and the police
were asking all kind of questions that Ladelle didn't want to answer.
He gave them his cousin's name instead of Peties; he knew if blue
and white ran his name they'd see a warrant pending. Ladelle rode
in the ambulance with Petie and Lou followed in the Hummer. He
called Renee on his cell phone and filled her in on what was happening.

Kalif was looking out the window when the ambulance and
three police cars had pulled up around ten to eleven. He smiled at
the scene. "You don't want no problems with Harlem, you don't want
no problems..." he rapped. He called out to BJ and Will, and they all
watched as the EMTs strapped Petie to the stretcher and pulled off.

Kalif knew the white Hummer parked down the street from

somewhere. He thought it might have belonged to one of Rasheed's peeps. Rasheed was Kalif's older brother. He had more props than a stage play, so Kalif wasn't worried about anything....

Kalif's guns went off, and niggas in the hood knew that. They used to call him 'Wild Child' when he was younger. Now at twenty-four he was even wilder. He had braids down his back and a basketball player's body. He was slim and tall with thick eyebrows. Young girls loved him. They all said he had a big dick, and Kalif was well aware of it. His anaconda was his pride and joy.

Chapter
Eleven

Venus and Share lay down to get some rest and the fellas began talking about their game plan. Will decided that Share should stay downtown in her getaway co-op just in case some drama broke out. The fellas all knew that shit was gonna jump off behind this. They didn't care; ride or die. Kalif and BJ placed calls to their peeps and told them what was what. They agreed to stay at Share's just in case niggas wanted to act up. It was about to go down.

Renee rushed to get dressed. She couldn't believe that Petie had gotten jumped; niggas knew better than that. She asked the Hispanic lady who lived next door if she could she keep an eye on Darnell and Dante. She didn't go into detail; the situation was none of her business. She caught a cab to Columbia Presbyterian on 168th and Broadway. She saw Lou's Hummer double-parked and rushed through the emergency door. She'd almost forgotten to pay the cab driver.

Porscha and Giselle were in bed when the phone rang. It was Renee calling to tell Giselle about Petie. She told her the sketchy details she knew and that he was at Columbia Presbyterian. Giselle jumped up, unstrapped her dildo and got dressed. She told Porscha what had happened and that she would call her when she got to the hospital. Like Renee, she couldn't believe that her Uncle Petie had gotten jumped. Petie and Giselle had always been close, and when her mother, Petie's sister, passed away, they became even closer. Giselle loved him more than anything. She called Renee and told her she was fifteen minutes away in a cab.

Derek, LeRoy and Freestyle got to Share's brownstone at eleven-thirty, and Will and BJ went down an opened the apartments on the first floor for them. They all admired the big screen TV, stereo system and leather sofa bed in the living room before sitting around the coffee table and pulling out their phillies. "Now what's good?" Derek said throwing four dimes on the table.

Kalif filled his boys in on everything. BJ told them that Petie's truck was still outside and that he had thrown his keys down the sewer. They all laughed, and Derek got up to look out the window. He recognized Petie's truck. "Yo, what's that cat's name?" he asked, already knowing the answer.

"Some faggot-ass name...Petie or some shit," Will replied. Derek lit up his blunt and told them what he knew about Petie. Petie had come through 130th and Fifth Avenue with three other cats causing ruckus. He told these kids they couldn't put work out there

unless they were gonna pay them rent. When Beans, the nigga who ran shit, showed up, the kids told him that Petie came through and took their work and left. Beans bitched up and moved his work to Park Avenue and 128th Street. Beans wasn't soft, but he didn't want any beef with Petie.

Kalif called his brother, Rasheed, and told him what went down and why. Rasheed remained quiet as he listened to the details. Kalif told him about the white Hummer.

"Listen, I know them cats. Big Lou is my man. He gonna fall back after I holla at him. The other cat was probably this nigga, Ladelle, from the Polo Grounds. Him and Petie is mad tight. He ain't gonna be trying to hear nothing. Did the nigga see ya'll before he went down?" Rasheed asked. Kalif told him Petie had seen them before they stomped him, but he might not remember.

"And who gives a fuck what that nigga remembers? He wanted it, I gave it. That's it and that's all," Kalif said taking a pull on his blunt. They talked a little while longer, and Kalif gave his brother Share's number and hung up. Then he told his team what Rasheed had told him.

"I don't give a fuck about that nigga's status," BJ said passing the blunt to Will. "Buttercup niggas want to run up on women. Run up on me, dog," he said patting his chest.

The phone rang and Derek picked it up. It was Porscha, wanting to know what had happened. "That gay bitch being nosy," he said to Will.

"Who the fuck you calling bitch, little boy?" Porscha yelled through the phone.

"You, bitch!" Derek screamed into the receiver. "Take your pussy-eating ass to the dentist and get the hairs out your teeth! He slammed the phone down, hoping that she would call back. He didn't like gay women, especially aggressors. His shorty had left him for an aggressor, and ever since then he had it out for all of them.

The fellas decided to go to Shaolin the next day to get some burners. Freestyle had a team out there with heavy artillery. He'd made one phone call and they told him they'd set him out. BJ said he couldn't take off from work tomorrow, but he could leave early. They'd all ride to Shaolin in two vehicles and pick up their business. The jump-off was now in progress.

Giselle arrived at the hospital, and when she saw Renee she ran up to her and hugged her. They both began to cry. Ladelle was talking to the doctor and Lou was sitting with his head in his hands. They were both in total shock; this shit just couldn't be happening to their partner.

The doctor told Renee that Petie had fluid on his brain and some inflammation. He had four broken ribs, a few missing teeth and the side of his skull was cracked. The doctor said he would survive and that she could see him after surgery. Petie was in critical condition, and the chances of him being the same were slim to none.

Ladelle went outside to smoke a cigarette and Lou followed him. Neither one of them spoke; they were weighing the severity of Petie's condition. Ladelle remembered that when they got Petie to the ER and took off his clothes, he didn't have any keys on him.

Ladelle puffed on his cigarette, and he now recalled that Petie had eight hundred dollars in his pants pocket. His burner was in the inside pocket of his coat and he didn't have his ice on when they got to the hospital. The doctor had given Ladelle his wedding band because his finger had been fractured.

"Something is funny 'bout this shit," Ladelle said putting out his cigarette. He told Lou about the pieces he had put together and the pieces that were missing. They agreed that it sounded like some kind of setup. "First of all, if the nigga had beef we'd know about it, and second of all, how could he have beef outside that bitch's house and she not know about it?" Ladelle added. He'd already figured out what really happened. He told Lou about Petie seeing the young boy driving her car and going in her house with the keys. They were both thinking the same thing. Lou went to get the Hummer and Ladelle went back to the waiting room to sit with Giselle. He knew that Giselle's wife was Share's friend, but that was about to change.

Chapter Twelve

The fellas were on their way back to the city from Shaolin. Venus called BJ, asking him his whereabouts; when she woke up to use the bathroom he wasn't there, and she became worried. He told her he had to make a run with the crew and would be back shortly. It was already going on three a.m. and he wanted to get at least two hours of sleep. Will asked if Share was awake and BJ said that Venus told him she wasn't. Venus told BJ to hurry up and get back.

When they got to 142nd and Amsterdam, Kalif spotted the white Hummer. "Oh, these niggas want it at three in the morning. I'ma have them yawnin'," he said before jumping out of Will's Durango along with Will, BJ and Derek. They all walked up 142nd Street toward Amsterdam. LeRoy and Freestyle had already driven around the block and came up behind the Hummer from

Amsterdam. LeRoy strapped his burner to his waist and put a razor in his mouth. They were parked by a phone booth where they could see everything, and they waited for whoever was in the Hummer to get out. BJ, Will, Kalif and Derek had now stopped in front of Share's building and sat on the steps.

Lou and Ladelle had already seen the four cats approaching from Convent Avenue, and Lou told Ladelle about the two cats parked behind them now. Ladelle looked back and smirked. "Oh, these young cats trying to snuff us. What you think?"

"I think we need to holla at the wolves and get crumped," Lou replied. Ladelle made a phone call, uttered a couple of words and hung up. He asked Lou if he was holding heat as he put a clip in his burner. Just as he finished putting the clip in, a Range Rover turned the corner and pulled up right beside them. Lou lowered his window and exchanged words with the driver. The Range cruised down to Convent, turned the corner and disappeared.

Kalif and his team saw the whole scenario. They'd been drinking and were now ready to do the damn thing. "Niggas trying to ambush us, son. Believe me when I tell you. I seen shit like this happen before," Kalif told his partners. He put out his cigarette and threw his beer bottle at the Hummer. The bottle hit the hood and busted.

"Let's get it crumped, my niggas," Will said. Before they could get in the middle of the street, Ladelle licked off two shots. One hit a pole and the other hit a parked car. Kalif opened up on the Hummer windows as the Range Rover came speeding down the block. Three cats jumped out on them, blazing heat. Freestyle and Derek had managed to pull Lou out the driver's seat and put two in him, while the cats in the Range Rover continued licking off mad shots. The whole block was being shot up. Car alarms were going off and a siren could be heard from not too far away. People were ducking behind anything and everything and creeping low alongside parked cars. Will and Kalif caught one of the cats from the Range and beat him down, causing everyone in the truck to scatter. Finally, one kid jumped back in the Range and before he could close the door, BJ ran up on him and put an ice pick in his neck. "Drive safely, punk," he said and pushed his head into the steering wheel. The sirens were getting louder and the fellas broke north. They didn't want to get caught running around, so they hurried back to the ground floor of Share's brownstone and stayed low.

Share and Venus had been awakened by the gunfire. They watched the shootout with their mouths open from the front window. Share couldn't believe what she was seeing. Not only was Petie's truck still outside, but Lou's Hummer was also there and some other truck in the middle of the street. It looked like a cowboy movie. They watched in horror as Derek put the heat to Lou's chest and hit him two times. Venus pulled Share away from the window and started getting dressed when they heard the fellas run inside....

Ladelle had managed to stay low during the shootout. He was not about to jump out when Lou was snatched out the Hummer. *Oh, shit,* he thought. Luckily they didn't see him, or he would've gotten done, too. He slid out from the driver's side and ducked down behind the Hummer. He felt Lou's neck for a pulse. It was faint, but at least he had one. "Hold on, nigga," he said as Lou began to moan. This was some drama for real. Ladelle had never planned for it to

come to this. He couldn't believe those young cats had ambushed them. He made it to Convent Avenue and ducked beside a van as two police cars sped by and turned up 142nd toward Amsterdam. When he got to 145th Street and Convent Avenue he hailed a cab.

Porscha called Share to find out what the fuck was going on. Venus answered the phone and told her they couldn't talk right now. Porscha was still talking when Venus hung up the phone. When she realized that no one was at the other end of the line, she panicked. She got dressed and put Diamond and Bullet in her minivan and headed over to Share's. She knew something was wrong when Share told her earlier that she had trouble with Petie. But when Giselle rushed out to the hospital, Porscha realized that shit was serious. She knew Petie was flip mode, but what could have happened that he was in the hospital, and how was Share involved? Porscha wondered if maybe Petie had hit Share, and she tried to defend herself and something went wrong.... *No, that wasn't it,* she thought. *And Giselle, how would she feel about all of this?* Giselle was one of those people who believed with all her heart that blood is thicker than water; no matter what, you always ride with your fam, whether they're right or wrong. Porscha prayed that whatever it was, it wouldn't affect their relationship. She said a silent prayer and hoped that God was listening.

Chapter
Thirteen

The block looked like something from a Bruce Willis movie. The entire area was sealed off, and cops were everywhere. There were ambulances and EMT workers, and a news van was giving live footage of the scene. Uniformed and undercover cops were marking shell cases from bullets that were fired. A body was put on a stretcher and rolled to an awaiting ambulance. Fingerprints were being taken off the Range Rover, as the dead man lay up against the steering wheel with the ice pick in his neck. The police asked the neighborhood residents if any one of them had seen or could identify any of the parties involved.

Porscha decided that she'd wait to speak to Share. It was obvious from the scene that whatever happened was the result of a little more than beef. Share had lied to her, but now was not the time

to find out what had really occurred. Whatever went down, Porscha knew that things were about to get even uglier.

Ladelle made it home. He had been hit in the shoulder, and he was in so much pain he thought he would pass out. He hadn't felt it before because his adrenaline was so high. He called his mother upstairs, waking her from a peaceful sleep, and ran up three flights. She was a nurse and would know what to do. She was surprised to see her son in this condition at four-thirty in the morning. She wanted to ask him what had happened, but instead she went to work on the wound. And since she didn't ask any questions, Ladelle didn't offer any information.

He felt bad about leaving Lou, but the last thing he needed was the police asking him questions while he stood over his man's body. He prayed that Lou was all right, even though he doubted it.

Ladelle's mind began to race. As his mother nurtured his shoulder, trying to find out exactly where the bullet was lodged, he was making plans. *Time to call in the reinforcements*, he thought.

Renee and Giselle got back to the house, and Renee explained to her Hispanic neighbor next door what had happened. She apologized for taking so long. Darnell and Dante had slept through everything, and Renee decided that it was best to wait until they woke up to let them know about their father. She wouldn't send them to school today, but she would send them to their grandmother's house.

Giselle called Ladelle and he filled her in on everything that happened and who he thought was the cause of it. Giselle was vexed after hearing that her wife's friend had started all this bullshit. She was the reason her uncle was laid up in the critical care unit fighting for his life. Giselle would see that bitch Share and put the beats on her fa sho.

She called Porscha and blasted her for not telling her the truth. As far as Giselle was concerned, she knew something from the jump. She remembered when Porscha had made that phone call and said something about 'beef.' Porscha tried to explain to Giselle that she didn't think it was that serious or she would have told her.

"Bitch, anything regarding my uncle is serious. And you laid up with me all fucken night and ain't tell me shit. Now what the fuck am I supposed to think?"

"But Giselle—"

"Shut the fuck up...so now I'm supposed to believe you wasn't protecting your bird friends?!" Giselle shrieked. If she was there with Porscha she would have taken her head off.

"All I'm saying is that—"

"Bitch, you ain't saying shit!" Giselle said cutting her off again and then pressing the *off* key on her phone. She turned around and saw Renee standing there watching her. She wondered how much of the conversation she had heard. Oh, well. It really didn't matter anyway. She had shit on the brain, and she didn't care what Renee heard or didn't hear.

Porscha was crying so hard that her head began to hurt.

This could not be happening to her. Everything in her life was going right, and now this dumb shit. She couldn't wait to talk to Share and Venus. *Them bitches is the cause of all this anyway*, she thought. If Giselle left her behind this bullshit, she would just die. She wouldn't be able to go on without her.

Porscha went into the bathroom and washed her face. Her eyes were swollen and she had a nose full of boogies. She looked and felt a mess. She knew what she needed...she'd be all right.

She went to the store and bought a six-pack of beer. *Thank God for twenty-four-hour stores*. When she got back home she checked to see if Giselle had called—she hadn't. It was daybreak and normally she would be getting ready for work, but not today. Today she was relapsing. She didn't want to call her sponsor and she didn't want to make a meeting. She just wanted to use.

Porscha called her job and said she wouldn't be in today because of a family emergency. The counselor on duty assured her that she would let the morning shift know, and she told Porscha she hoped everything turned out all right.

Porscha never missed any days at work, so no one was likely to suspect anything. She opened one of the beers and took a swig.

Share had just arrived at her condo on Seventy-Fourth Street when the phone rang. It was Venus, making sure she got there safely. She and BJ were on their way home, trying to act like nothing had happened. Venus told her about how the fellas had gone out the back door of the brownstone, went through an opening and came out on 141st Street. From there they caught cabs in different directions.

Share was concerned about all the drama that had been brought to her house. Why did those niggas have to do that shit at her crib? Now it was all going to come back to her. And she knew she'd have to call the police eventually because Ladelle wasn't going to let it rest.

Share called the hospital to find out how serious Petie's condition was. She was told that he was in the ICU and could only have visitors from immediate family. She decided to wait for Will so they could sort things out.

Kalif hollered at his brother to let him know that they had set it on the niggas in the white Hummer. Rasheed was not happy; he had already told Kalif to let him handle it, but Kalif hadn't listened. And now there was no telling what would happen now.

Kalif turned on the news and was surprised to see a live broadcast from 142nd Street. He called BJ and Will to tell them that they had made the news.

"Yeah, my niggas. Throw your guns up and hit the news. Channel 7 is uptown. They probably got that shit on 1010 Wins, too," Kalif said, not realizing how serious the matter was. The neighbors would probably start talking and the police would be snatching up anybody moving.

"Fuck TV, dun. We don't need that shit. Some old lady probably sayin' she seen this and seen that. Niggas is still on paper. I ain't trying to catch no new charges. We just gonna walk softly and see what them cats gon' do," Will told Kalif. Kalif was a loose cannon. He

was already thinking about part two. He didn't give a fuck about the nosy neighbors or what his brother had said. Fuck them, and fuck Will, too, if he wanted to bitch up. Anybody who wanted the business was gonna get it.

Chapter Fourteen

Petie had just come in from therapy and was watching the news. Renee had gone out again this morning and he was starting to wonder about where she was spending her time. Ever since he came home from the hospital he noticed that she went out every morning at the same time. The only time she stayed home was on weekends. He wondered if it was always like that or because he wasn't the same. Petie wasn't usually home in the morning, so he didn't know if this was something new or if she had *been* doing it. Ladelle called him last night and said he would drop by after his therapy. Shit just wasn't the same.

Petie's speech was getting better and his memory was coming back little by little. He felt like some type of weirdo. It took him a long time to get his thoughts together and he couldn't concentrate

like he used to. Those young bloods had done him dirty. He couldn't wait until he got back to his normal self. The doctor told him his condition wasn't permanent and that he'd be *normal* again, as long as he kept up his therapy.

Petie turned off the news and tried to remember the face of the nigga who had pulled out on him. That was the last thing he remembered. That nigga would be the first one he got at.

Renee's lover had his face buried so deep in her black box that she thought he was going to suffocate. She arched her back, as her spasms came quick and long. He began kissing his way up her thighs now and playing with her nipples. She wanted to suck his dick. She loved sucking his dick, especially right before he entered her. She told him to stand up on the side of the bed and put one leg up on the mattress. He was rock hard and his balls were dangling between his legs. She tickled his balls with the tip of her tongue and pulled on his hairs with her teeth. Then she turned him around and spread his cheeks and started licking his asshole. He liked that shit. Renee put her face in his ass and began sucking his asshole until his knees buckled. She turned him back around and ran her tongue along his dick as if she were eating an icecream cone. Renee deep-throated him until his head was at the back of her throat. She sucked it like a Tootsie Roll Pop until she tasted his pre-cum. He lay on his back and Renee got on top and straddled him. He gripped her ass and spread her cheeks, putting his finger in her booty hole. She leaned forward and he put her titty in his mouth. He finger-fucked her ass until she couldn't take it anymore....she busted off, slid down between his legs and sucked him some more. She then turned around doggy style and he beat himself on her cheeks. Facing him again now, she sucked and licked him until he exploded on her chest. She rubbed his milk against her breasts and lay down, never once thinking about Petie. Her lover was the only thing on her mind the whole time, and being home before the kids came from school was all the mattered.

Giselle went into the bank and asked about opening an account. She really just wanted to see if Venus was there—she was. Giselle left the bank and waited across the street. Finally, Venus came out and went to a coffee stand near the bank. Giselle walked across the street to the stand and stood behind her. When Venus turned around, she snuffed her with the razor that was between her index and middle fingers. The Arabian man who owned the stand stared in disbelief.

Giselle went to the corner and caught a cab, not caring whether or not anyone had identified her. Everything in her world had fallen apart. Her uncle Petie was like some kind of vegetable, and Lou, who was *like* an uncle to her, was now buried. On top of all that, Porscha had started shooting dope again, so fuck that. Nothing mattered to her anymore, and as soon as she dealt with Share, she was going to head down south and lay low. But first she had one more thing to do before she bounced.

Share was on her way to the post office when BJ called her from Harlem Hospital and told her that Venus had been attacked. He told her everything he knew and that the police had a description of the female suspect. He waited while Venus was being stitched up, and he was a mess by the time Share arrived. Share had never seen

him like this before, and she asked if maybe this was the result of the shootout. She knew Giselle was Petie's niece, and from the description BJ gave, it sounded like it was her who had cut Venus. Share decided to go to the police. Fuck that; her friend was getting stitches in her face and she knew she'd be next. Oh, hell no! She had a license to carry a weapon and she would start packing it. *A bitch wanna run around with razors...okay. She better pray that her razor can stop bullets,* she thought.

Ladelle picked Darnell and Dante up from school and took them to get some Haagen Daz's ice cream. They ate it on sugar cones with sprinkles on top. Petie was sitting outside in the truck playing music when they pulled up. Ladelle took Darnell and Dante inside and came back outside to get in the truck with Petie. They talked for a little while before Petie went inside the house.

Renee was telling the kids to take off their school clothes and get ready to do their homework. Petie noticed that she was in a good mood and he wondered if she was cheating on him; she was just a little too carefree, and she hadn't given him any pussy since way before he went into the hospital. He couldn't even *remember* the last time he fucked her.

Petie sat at the table with his little men and watched them do their homework. They had been so helpful since he came home...at least they weren't acting any differently toward him. They knew their father would be back to his old self in no time.

Share pulled up to the front of her brownstone. She and Will had decided to stay back uptown. She noticed the Durango parked not too far away, so he was already there. She backed into the parking spot and grabbed her briefcase from off the back seat. She didn't see Giselle coming toward her from across the street, and when she dropped her keys and bent down to pick them up, Giselle kicked her to the ground. Share had a Timberland boot print on her Armani suit, and before she could get up, Giselle began kicking her in the face. Share reached up and punched Giselle in the jaw and then managed to bite her on the ankle. When Giselle bent down to release her ankle from Share's grip, Share hit her square in the nose. Giselle stumbled, trying to focus after getting what felt like a head butt. Share was on her feet now. She kicked off her heels and threw up her hands. "Bring it, bitch. Let me see what you got, you dildo-wearin' bitch!" Share was in a boxing stance. Giselle wasn't aware of the fact that Share had practiced kickboxing in her early twenties and had skills. She charged Share and tried to take her off her feet. Share kicked Giselle and stepped back to regain her balance. Giselle began yelling and cursing at Share. Her nose was still hurting, and she bent down and threw dirt in Share's eyes.

All the commotion downstairs made Will go to the window. He saw Giselle pulling out a razor. Share raised her arm to protect her face and the razor cut her suit. She could see blood coming through her sleeve. She managed to duck and miss Giselle's next attempt to cut her face. Will came flying out the door and bum-rushed Giselle. They both landed on the ground, and the razor flew

out of Giselle's hand. Share grabbed her bag and pulled a .22 out on Giselle. Will got to his feet and yanked Giselle up by the throat. Giselle snuffed him, catching him on the side of his head. He stumbled and she hit him again. Will body-slammed her to the ground and then walked toward Share to take the pistol from her. Her hand was shaking violently, and he didn't want her to pull the trigger by accident.

Will never saw Giselle when she got up to go and get her razor, which was a few feet away. She then came up behind him and sliced him across the back of his head. Suddenly two shots rang out. Giselle grabbed her stomach and collapsed to the ground, falling backwards. Share dropped the gun and fell to her knees crying. Giselle was now struggling to say something and Will, holding his head, turned around and bent down to listen to her closely as Share dialed 9-1-1 on her cell phone. "Die, you bitch," Giselle finally managed to spit out.

Will stood up straight and stared hatefully at her. "You die first, you wannabe nigga," he said before kicking her in the face and watching the blood gush out of her nose.

Chapter Fifteen

Renee and Petie were clearing the table after dinner when the 30th precinct called. They told him about his niece and that Share was taken into police custody. He couldn't believe it. His niece was dead, Lou was dead and he felt like dying. He called Ladelle and asked him to come and get him. He had to see his niece for himself. He didn't want to believe that she was dead...there was just no way; she was only twenty-six, so this had to be some kind of a mistake. Ladelle pulled up, and he and Petie went to identify the body.

Venus kept hearing Diamond barking. She knew Porscha was using again and wasn't taking Diamond out like she used to. She hadn't heard from Porscha since yesterday morning, and she wanted to

break the news to her about Giselle.

She knocked on Porscha's door, but there was no answer. Diamond was not only barking now; she was howling. Venus turned the knob and when the door opened, Diamond rushed downstairs like a bat out of hell. Venus called out to Porscha—no response. The apartment felt eerie and there was a stale smell. There were clothes lying about everywhere in the bedroom, and when Venus walked toward the bathroom she saw a foot. She knew it belonged to Porscha. She was afraid to open the door the rest of the way. When she got up the nerve, the weight of Porscha's body prevented her from doing so, and she turned and ran down the stairs, almost breaking her neck. She called an ambulance, but it was too late when it arrived; Porscha was already dead from a drug overdose.

Kalif was coming out of the Magic Johnson Theatre off of 125th Street with some chick from Atlanta. She was visiting New York for the weekend, and he was going to make sure he sent her back home with something to talk about.

They rented a room on 145th between Amsterdam and Broadway for four hours. Kalif dicked her down for an hour and a half. She was a cutie but her pussy stunk. He couldn't rock to that beat. Kalif told her he was going to get some cigs and a phillie. He never returned. *Take that fishy shit back to the ATL, ma.*

Kalif walked down 145th and started to cross St. Nicholas. He was thinking about going to see his peeps over on Bradhurst when he saw a familiar looking truck. Before he could cross the street, Ladelle and Biz came at him. Kalif did not expect to see these niggas now. He did the only thing he could do—run. Ladelle screamed out to the Jamaicans on Edgecombe to grab the bumba-clot. One of the dreads who'd heard Ladelle clipped Kalif as soon as he turned the corner. Kalif tripped and landed face first, chipping his fronts, and his gums and hands were bloody. Biz pulled out a billy club and caught Kalif across the jaw. Ladelle threw Kalif through the windshield of a parked car, and broken glass sprayed everywhere. The corner was so crowded it looked like someone was filming a video. Ladelle grabbed Kalif by his braids and threw him back on the sidewalk, where Petie stomped him with steel-toed toes. It was a wrap. They headed back to Petie's truck and left Kalif for dead.

Petie was starting to feel like his old self again, even though he had-n't gotten back behind the wheel; Ladelle was pushing his truck until he was ready to drive again. Still, Petie knew he was blessed to be alive. As far as those young niggas were concerned, Ladelle would even the score. That was his motherfucken man.

Petie said a silent prayer for Big Lou. Don't worry, my nigga; your death won't be in vain...yours either, Giselle.

Share couldn't wait to get in the shower. The police had let her go and said that no charges were currently being filed against her. Luckily, one of her nosy, elderly neighbors was able to give the police a report of what she saw. They were satisfied for now because it sounded like Share was just defending herself. She went to the hospital and had ten stitches put in the razor cut on her arm that Giselle had given her when she tried to cut her face. Good thing she had blocked it, or it would have been her cheekbone getting stitches.

Will had left her a note saying that he was at his mother's house and to call as soon as she got in. The police had told Share that a squad car would be patrolling her block, and if she saw anything suspicious to call 9-1-1 immediately. They gave her protection because of her credentials; she was a taxpayer, had no criminal background and owned two franchises. Yeah, the police believed her story. She never meant to kill Giselle; she was simply defending herself. And more than anything, she wanted this nightmare to be over.

Renee got the kids ready for school and woke Petie up for his therapy. She showered, had breakfast and waited for her lover to call. He didn't, so she called him. He told her he'd see her tomorrow morning. *Okay, see you tomorrow*, she thought.

Ladelle was at his ex-girl's house. He was thinking about them getting back together for good this time. He missed her, but she was always complaining about his lifestyle. She was a good girl; she was in college, worked part time and didn't run the streets. He needed a chick like that. Since he had to pick up Darnell and Dante from school soon, he'd just stay there until she came in from her class.

He decided to tell his sidekick that it was over. He wanted

something more than what she had to offer. Yeah, he would be with his secret lover one last time, and then he would dead it.

Will was leaving his mother's house when BJ called him to tell him about Kalif. Kalif was at Rasheed's house. They were going to take him to St.Lukes; he had four chipped teeth and a couple of scrapes. Nothing appeared to be broken, but they didn't know yet. Kalif had told BJ about how he was crossing St. Nicholas, spotted that burgundy truck and niggas started chasing him.

Will wasn't really feeling this shit anymore; it had been going on for two months already. He had to report to parole in the morning and he needed his rest. But he understood why BJ was still holding on to *his* beef; Venus had gotten her face sliced. However, he wasn't trying to get caught up with any new charges. Enough was enough already; let the score be settled. On the other hand, niggas jumping out on Kalif had started up more shit now. As he turned the corner, he realized that it wasn't over...ride or die.

Venus examined her stitches in the mirror. Luckily for her there were only ten of them. The doctor had done a pretty good job, but she began to worry about the mark she might have after the stitches healed. She might have to get cosmetic surgery. Share had assured her that they would find the best doctor to do the work, no matter what the cost.

Share was in Venus' living room watching Diamond with her

new puppies. She wondered what it felt like to be a mother. Now that Petie was out of her life, maybe she and Will could start a family.

Share and Venus were packing up Porscha's things later on when Share came across a photo album and began to cry. *Porscha was so pretty. Why did she have to die like that? Why did everything seem to fall apart all at once?*

Venus said she couldn't stay in the apartment; she felt like Porscha was still there and her soul was not at rest. She remembered finding her body and breaking down in tears. She and Share embraced and tried to comfort one another. Before leaving the apartment, they said a prayer for Porscha. "God bless her soul," they said.

Chapter Sixteen

Petie was asleep when Ladelle and Biz rang the bell. They came in, sat on the sofa and told him how they'd caught another one of the kids on Edgecomb. Petie wanted to get back to the streets. He couldn't stand it, being in the house all the time waiting for his body to heal.

"How's that therapy coming along?" Biz asked Petie. Just looking at Petie made him want to catch *all* of those punks, one by one.

"It's getting easier. I'm just anxious to get back to my old self, you know what I mean?" Petie's speech was better now; his words were no longer slurred like before. It was just a matter of time. He had to be patient.

They decided to go for a ride. Ladelle told Petie that he had

seen Des. "She looked fucked up, dick. She smoking that shit. Bitch smoked her ass away. Her skin looked fucked up, too."

"Yeah, I knew she was hitting the stem. Last time I hollered at her she didn't look right to me. I threw her some crills and bounced," Petie said while remembering how good she sucked dick.

They stopped on 126th and Morningside, and Biz got out of Petie's truck and strolled into a building to check on something. A black and gold SUV pulled up behind them. Rasheed got out and opened up on the truck. Biz was still inside the building when he heard gun play. He ran outside and returned fire. Petie was okay, but Ladelle had been hit in the shoulder. Biz jumped back in the truck and they took off after Rasheed. Rasheed knew he had hit them. He knew that at least one person was in the truck; he couldn't see because of the tinted windows. He sped down 125th Street and turned on Fifth Avenue. He parked his truck, jumped out and ran into a building. He made a phone call and got the voicemail. Frustrated, he put his burner away and went back outside. He walked to Park Avenue and used the pay phone. He called 9-1-1 and reported a shooting involving a burgundy truck on 126th Street. He knew the police would snatch all those niggas up, whoever was in it. Before Rasheed got back to the building, Petie's truck drove up alongside him and he was put to rest. He never lived to know if the police picked them up or not.

Ladelle was bleeding badly. He would have to go to the emergency room this time. It wasn't like previously, when his mother was able to do some homemade surgery and removed the bullet before stitching him up.... His side was burning. He lay across the back seat as Biz drove to Harlem Hospital.

After being released from the hospital, Kalif couldn't wait to get uptown. One of his chicks called him and told him that Rasheed was dead. Kalif screamed at the cab driver, telling him to hurry the fuck up. Finally he got to Harlem Hospital, where Rasheed had been pronounced dead on arrival. Kalif punched a window, shattering it to pieces. A few nurses who were standing nearby tried to calm him down, but it was useless.

Kalif called LeRoy and told him to come and get him. He lit a cigarette and stared up at the sky as he waited for him outside the hospital's front entrance.... *Niggas killed my brother. Shit is getting critical*, he thought.

LeRoy pulled up and hopped out of his Highlander, leaving it doubled-parked. Neither one of them knew what to say. "Don't worry; it ain't over. Niggas still want the business. Well, we gon' keep givin' it to 'em," Leroy finally said. The look in Kalif's eyes was homicidal. He was turning into a madman. He knew what had to be done, and they were going to do it.

Biz pulled up behind Harlem Hospital, unaware that Kalif and LeRoy were parked on the opposite side. He helped Ladelle into the emergency room, and Petie followed.

Biz walked outside and got back into Petie's truck. He was going to drop off the burner he was carrying; he didn't want the nurses asking questions, even though they had already put a story together.

Biz got to the light and noticed the police looking at the truck. It had bullet holes in it, and they would definitely want to know what had happened. The light changed and Biz took off, making sure to stay within the speed limit. The police turned on their siren and signaled for him to pull over. With their guns drawn, they approached the truck and ordered Biz to keep his hands where they could see them. Biz didn't move. His heat was right next to him on the front seat. He had his hands on the steering wheel, and one officer approached him on the passenger side of the truck. The door was locked, and the tints on the window kept the officer from seeing the gun. Biz reached for his heat and fired through the passenger side window, hitting the officer in the chest. The other officer ran up and opened fire, and Biz died with the burner still in his hand.

Kalif and Leroy decided to hit Petie and his crew at home. "I don't give a fuck who in there—grandmother, aunt, kids...I don't give a fuck. Everybody gon' catch a bullet," Kalif said. Yeah, he was definitely a wild child.

LeRoy needed to drop Kalif off to go and take care of some business. He would stand by him, but right now he had some other shit to tend to. He let Kalif out of the Highlander and headed to the Bronx.

Share and Will were back at her brownstone when she decided she wanted the beige puppy that looked like Bullet. Will turned on the news, and it was being reported that a police officer had been shot in front of McDonald's on Lenox Avenue. The assailant was killed and the owner of the truck had reportedly been in a couple of shootouts that led to one man being treated at Harlem Hospital. The police were waiting to question them both. Share looked at Will. They were both thinking the same thing. Will hastily called BJ to make sure he was okay. He panicked when he got the voicemail. He didn't yet know that Kalif's brother, Rasheed, had been killed by Petie's crew. He just knew that BJ was still hung up on everything that had happened.

Share was about to call Venus when the phone rang. It was BJ. The cell was on vibrate, and he didn't feel it when Will had called. He said he was fine and on his way home. He would call when he got there.

Renee and the boys were eating when Petie called from the precinct. He couldn't talk long, so he just told Renee the basics. The police had impounded his truck as evidence, Biz had gotten killed by the cops and Ladelle was in the hospital undergoing surgery. The bullet that hit him in the side had moved, and emergency surgery had to be performed before it got to his spine. In the midst of it all, one of the doctors in the ER notified the police that he was a gunshot victim.

Petie said the police had arrested him because they'd gotten a 9-1-1 call that identified his truck in the shootout, although he really felt he was being held because of his priors. He was sure it wasn't because he was on parole. When he was in the hospital Renee had contacted his parole officer, and when he came home and started therapy, he had given him some room. Therefore, Petie knew that his being on parole wasn't an issue. It was definitely his rap sheet.

Renee could hardly think with Ladelle in surgery. *What if he doesn't make it?* Oh, she didn't want to think about that. She had to stop thinking negative thoughts. But she couldn't bare the thought of going on without him. They had been lovers for over a year now...all the romantic times, the erotic moments, the never-ending orgasms...no, this couldn't be happening. She went back to the table and stared at her plate of food. She didn't want to eat; she wanted to be in Ladelle's arms.

Renee was at the precinct waiting to get Petie's property. The officer at the desk was rude, as were all the other ones who had walked by her cutting their eyes. *Fuck y'all*, she said to herself. Her world was falling apart, and she really didn't care what they thought. She just wanted to get to the hospital to see Ladelle.

Chapter seventeen

Ladelle woke up with his ankle cuffed to the hospital bed. *What the fuck?* Yeah, he knew why he was cuffed. He remembered the under-covers saying they wanted to ask a few questions before he passed out. That was the setup right there, and now his ass was cuffed to a bed.

He pushed the button on the side of his bed, and a West Indian nurse came into his room. He covered the lower part of his body so she wouldn't get a glimpse of the python. The last thing he wanted was for her to go into shock and pass out. At his request, she brought him something to drink and told him that his mother and girlfriend were waiting to see him.

They entered his room with flowers and get-well cards. His mother approached his bed and leaned over and kissed him on the

forehead. His ex-girl, Lydia, gave him a peck on the lips and pulled up a chair alongside the bed. Ladelle told them about how Biz got out of the truck and some kid just started shooting at them. His mother told him she had spoken to Petie. Petie was going to say he let Biz use the truck for a couple of hours, and the next thing he knew they were arresting him at the hospital. She told Ladelle to tell the police he was a robbery victim, or that he'd gotten caught in some sort of crossfire. That way they wouldn't connect Ladelle to the shooting that left Rasheed dead. They didn't know if it would work, but it sounded good. Ladelle's mother prepared to leave and told him she'd be back after taking care of some business.

Renee saw Ladelle's mother leaving the hospital, and she felt glad about getting some time alone with him. She got a visitor's pass and headed to his room. Before opening the door she heard him say, "...and I should've never left you to begin with, Lydia. You know you my heart. When all this shit is over with, we gonna try again."

"Okay, but this little *accident* don't interfere with your per- formance, daddy? Because if it does, I'm gonna have to lay you back and ride you like a rollercoaster until you get better," Lydia said before vividly describing to Ladelle all the new positions they would have to try.

Renee opened the door and walked into the room. She kissed Ladelle on the forehead and acted as if she didn't even see Lydia. She removed her coat and took Ladelle's hand. If Lydia didn't know any better, she would have thought that Renee was fucking Ladelle. Lydia knew she was Petie's wife, but she didn't understand why she was being so affectionate toward Ladelle. Ladelle, feeling a little uncomfortable now, sat up in the bed and started to introduce them.

"I know who she is," Renee said turning her back toward Lydia.

"Excuse me," Lydia said. "I'm gonna step out and leave you two to talk. I'll be back in ten minutes, daddy." As Lydia was leaving the room, Renee handed her her coat and said, "It's cold outside. Take your time."

Ladelle got right to the point when the door closed behind Lydia. "Check this out: that's my girl, Renee, and all that attitude you just gave her, I ain't like that shit one bit. In any event, me and you is dead. Too much shit is going on right now and a nigga is ready to settle down, so..."

Renee had put on her coat, picked up her pocketbook and headed toward the door before Ladelle finished his statement. "Dead, huh? I'll show you dead. Then I'll show that chicken head your bite marks on my thighs." She slammed the door and waited for Lydia to come off the elevator.

When Lydia stepped off the elevator, she was shocked to see Renee standing there. She was holding a cup of hot chocolate, preparing to get back to Ladelle's room, but the look on Renee's face said otherwise. Renee spit in Lydia's face and when she turned to walk away, Lydia threw the hot chocolate on her.

"You Payless-shoe-wearin', ninety-nine-cent-store-shop-pin', metro-card-usin' bitch!" Renee shouted and slapped Lydia into the nurses' station. The nurses backed away from the desk and

watched, waiting to see a fight. Lydia snatched off her coat and even though she couldn't fight, she threw up her hands like she could. Renee punched her, grabbed a handful of her hair and knotted her up. By this time security had come to the floor and escorted Renee out of the hospital.

When Lydia got back to the room, Ladelle looked at her like she had just stepped out of a wrestling ring. A nurse came into the room and gave her some A&D ointment for her scrapes and a busted lip. Lydia couldn't believe that Renee had jumped on her like that. She went to the mirror, put the ointment on her lip and tried to fix her weave. Renee had pulled out some of her tracks, and there were patches of hair missing in certain areas throughout her head. She looked a mess.

Ladelle picked up the hospital phone to call Renee and curse her out. He didn't know the bitch was psycho like that. *She gonna blow up my spot with that dumb shit.*

Ladelle couldn't get a word in; Renee was yelling at the top of her lungs, talking about how she was going to tell Petie this and tell him that. *What the fuck is wrong with her? Did she think that shit was gonna last forever?* Ladelle thought.

Renee was still riffin' when he hung up the phone. He looked at Lydia, who was searching around in her pocketbook for some glue to fix her tracks. Renee had fucked her up. Ladelle didn't know Renee had a knuckle game like that.

He laid back and looked at the cuff on his ankle. Shit was critical. The last few months had been nothing but drama. And now Renee wanted to tell Petie, his main man, that he had been digging her out. *What else could go wrong?* he thought.

Petie stood before the judge and was arraigned on two felony charges. Bail was a dead issue since he was on parole. Ladelle was also arraigned on charges at his hospital bed, being that he was in the truck when someone opened fire on them and the police report said that witnesses saw them return fire. However, the cops hadn't yet tied Rasheed's murder to Petie and Ladelle because Biz was in possession of the gun that killed him when the police shot him to death.

Petie's lawyer told him that he could be placed at the scene of the crime because of police witnesses. Petie didn't believe there were any witnesses; niggas in the hood minded their own business. He knew that was just a scare tactic. But he also knew that his priors would support the charges; his rap sheet was nothing but violence and gun play. He knew he was going up with a new number. But that didn't scare him. This would be his fourth state bid, and parole would just put his time on the back. He'd tell his lawyer on the next court date that he'd cop out to lesser charges because there was no way he was going to trial. Petie knew Ladelle would feel the same way. *Ain't no big deal*, he thought. As long as they weren't talking football numbers he'd do the time—easy.

Venus, Share, Will and BJ were at Share's brownstone watching the news. The reporter was giving continuing coverage involving the officer who had been shot. The bulletproof vest he wore saved his life. Meanwhile, charges were now being filed against Petie and Ladelle because the truck was registered in Petie's name, which made him an accessory to the murder of Rasheed Millen, and Ladelle's prints were found on the gun.

Venus turned the channel. She was tired of all the violence. She could have been dead, and Share could have been in jail for killing Giselle. *All this shit because of Petie. That nigga was bad news from day one*, she thought.

Venus never told Share about all the times Petie came to the bank and tried to hit on her. And she never told her about the time he grabbed her ass so hard that it hurt for a whole day. "When I'm done with Share, I'm coming after you," he'd always say. Venus gave Petie props on his good looks—his smile, his six-pack, the tattoos, his walk, side burns...everything. But his personality and his big ego made him ugly. Venus was happy he was locked up and out of her friend's life. Beside that, she and BJ's relationship had gotten stronger, and they were both relieved that all the drama was behind them.

They played scrabble and spades until late in the evening when Venus and BJ left to go home. Share and Will made love through the night and held each other in the darkness. *Yeah, everything is all right and back to normal*, Will thought. And he was where he wanted to be forever—in Share's world. Everything was everything.

The courtroom was packed. Petie was sentenced to three and a half to nine years, and Ladelle was sentenced to three to six years. It was all good; they had been blessed with so little time.

Renee brought Darnell and Dante to Rikers Island so they could see their father before he went up North. Petie was looking better and his scars were healing quickly. She would stand by him no matter what, but only for the sake of their sons.

Ladelle and Lydia had a small wedding while he was out on bail fighting the case. They made love all over the apartment the night before he turned himself in. Ladelle had told her the truth about he and Renee, and she forgave him. She just hoped that Petie never found out.

A count was taken and Petie got into the shower. Mike-Mike was already there. Petie walked up behind him, rubbed the soap between his ass cheeks and slid up in him. After a few moments Petie busted off and washed himself. Mike-Mike left the shower first, and then Petie dried off and went to his cell. He lay on his back and looked up at the ceiling. He thought of Share and smiled. He had big plans for her. *I'll be back*, he thought.

chapter Eighteen

Share and Pirate were on their way home from their nightly walk through Riverside Park. Most of the time he walked Share. He was three years old now, the first of Diamond and Bullet's litter. He had grown up to be a pretty dog, and he was strong.

Share stopped at the store to get some fruit juice and Pedigree. She crossed Amsterdam and stopped so Pirate could relieve himself. She enjoyed the breeze that was blowing and ran her fingers through her hair, never noticing the guy who was standing across the street in front of the pay phone. She still didn't notice him as he walked toward her because she had bent down to pick up Pirate's shit with the pooper-scooper.

"Excuse me, miss. You got a light?" he asked her. Share looked up and dropped the shit back on the ground. Pirate began to growl and bark. Share was scared. The last person she expected to see was Petie. Before she could say a word he said, "Yo, get your dog before I put a bullet in him." Sensing that something wasn't right, Pirate started to bark even louder. If it wasn't for his leash, he probably would have had Petie's neck between his teeth.

Share couldn't move. She knew Petie would kill Pirate, and God only knew what he would do to her. Petie had sent her hate-mail for the last two and a half years, and she kept every letter. She showed them to the District Attorney who had handled Petie's case. He assured her that they would notify her before his release, but they hadn't. Now he was standing right in front of her, and she was too scared to move.

"What do you want from me, Petie?" she asked him. Her fear was evident and there was a tremor in her voice. Petie didn't respond; he just looked at her, lit a cigarette and blew smoke in her face. He took another drag, blew smoke in Pirate's face and winked his eye at him. Pirate barked louder and began to jump at Petie. "I asked you a question, Petie. Please answer it. I mean, you got me standing here while you blow smoke in my face and give me dirty looks. What is it that you want?"

Petie dropped his cigarette to the ground. "You'll know what I want when I come for it," he said. He then bounced, leaving her wondering what the fuck he was talking about.

Petie had been home for a month, and that was the first time he let Share see him, even though he had seen her a couple of times. Renee had traded in the truck and bought a brand new Navigator, so Share didn't know what he was driving. When the police released the

truck to Renee while he was locked up, he had told her to get rid of it; it was bad luck.

Petie had gotten a kick out of the expression that appeared on Share's face when she saw him. It made him smile to see how shook she was. He'd told her in his letters that he was coming home to square shit off. *What, she didn't believe me? She took me for a joke or some shit? Maybe she thought I was bluffin'. I'll show you bluffin! She must've thought I was just trying to scare her. Nah, she started all of this drama, and I meant everything I said!* he thought. He remembered seeing Will pushing her Lexus and using the keys to her house, and Share barking at him like he was some fifteen-cent nigga when he called her and asked about it. Then she had him jumped, killed his niece and set up Lou and Ladelle, which led to Lou's death—not to mention his man, Biz. Yeah, she was the cause of everything. Petie decided that he'd play with her for a little while before putting her to rest. All of the things he had in store made his dick hard.

Shit had changed so much since before Petie got knocked. There were a bunch of new cats in the hood, and niggas who didn't know him acted like *he* was new. He had only done three years, but it seemed like more. He couldn't wait to get back in the game, even though it wouldn't be the same without his old team. They were the originals from back in the day, when they were all much younger and running shit. That seemed like a long time ago, but it wasn't. He just *had* to get on his feet again.

Petie got to his house, parked and sat behind the wheel. He began to think. There was so much he had to do. His sons were thirteen and fourteen now, and they were happy that he was home. Renee had faithfully made that trip up North twice a month so he could see his sons. They knew he was *Daddy,* but he hoped they weren't angry with him. The last thing he wanted to do was disappoint them.

"Dad, don't worry. We understand," Darnell always said. "We just want you home." Darnell was now the spitting image of Petie. Dante, on the other hand, favored Renee in complexion and features.

Petie locked the Navigator and went inside the house. Renee and Dante were on the living room couch watching TV and Darnell was on the phone, probably talking to some little girl. Petie went into the kitchen and took his plate out of the microwave. Renee would make a plate for him and put it in the microwave when he didn't make it home for dinner. Now, this was something new; before getting locked up, if he missed dinner he'd have to make his own plate.

Renee seemed different to him. She could still cook her ass off and took good care of the boys, but something wasn't the same about her.... He thought that maybe they could start off fresh. He didn't want to cause her any stress or pain; he just wanted to make shit right.

Renee got up from the couch and went into the bedroom. She took off her shorts and top and was putting on her nightgown when Petie came in and stood behind her. He started rubbing her shoulders and kissing the back of her neck. Renee turned around and returned his kisses. She wanted Petie to make love to her. In

some way or another she missed him. Petie sat on the edge of the bed and took off his clothes. Renee lay down and began massaging herself. She was moist and ready for penetration. Petie lay on top of her, and she opened up and let him in. She had forgotten how good her husband made her feel. His body was stronger and more toned than before. She dug her nails in his back as he stroked her. He pulled himself all the way out of her and teased her clit with the head of his dick. Petie slid his hands underneath her and spread her ass cheeks, now throwing himself deep inside of her. He stroked her until she came. Renee's muscles gripped him until he could no longer hold on. Finally, Petie busted off. He kissed Renee with so much passion that it felt like their first year together. He remembered how much he loved her and what he had put her through. He slid out of her and held her in his arms. "I promise you, Renee, I'm gonna fix everything that's wrong. Just gimme some time, ma. Ya heard?" he said.

"Just don't do anything that's gonna hurt us, Petie," she replied. Petie knew she was talking about illegal shit. He'd thought about getting a job and bringing home honest money; he wanted to set a good example for his sons. He still had a lot of years left on parole, and he damn sure didn't want any new numbers—not again. The thought of going back up North made him want to change his lifestyle and habits. No, he didn't want to do any more time. That was not in his plans. His only plan was getting even with Share so she could suffer and hurt like he did. And as long as he was alive, she would.

Renee put on her robe and told Darnell to get off the phone

and get ready for bed. Dante was in his room laying out his clothes for school the next day. Darnell was so much like Petie that it scared Renee. She didn't want him to make the same choices that his father had. He liked to draw, so Renee made sure he had all the materials he needed. She wanted the best for her sons, and she hoped that Petie would change so he could be a positive influence in their lives.

Chapter Nineteen

Lydia was cooking dinner when Ladelle came in from work. He had been home on work release for eight months. He had a board coming up and he prayed he made that board. This was his third state bid and he was hoping they didn't hit him. He was seven and zero now and doing everything he was supposed to do be doing. He had found a job as a cook in midtown and he was bringing home legal money. He saved every dime he made because Lydia was six months pregnant.

Ladelle had made up his mind that he was done with the game. There was no turning back; he had a child on the way and no matter what, he wanted to live to raise it. Lydia had stuck by him and every time she came to see him, she set him out so that his locker stayed full of everything. Yeah, Ladelle was done with the game and anything involving it.

Lydia called him into the kitchen to taste the pepper steak. "Is it too spicy?" she asked him.

"Nah, ma, its perfect. But put some more green peppers in it...wait, I'll cut some up. Have a seat and let daddy do this," Ladelle said kissing Lydia on the neck. In addition to cutting up more green peppers, he added red peppers, onions and added more seasoning to the pepper steak. Truth be told, Lydia couldn't cook for shit. She fucked up hard boiled eggs, burned the bagels, made the rice too mushy and the Kool-Aid too bitter. She was a danger to food, and Ladelle preferred that she just make toast.

Ladelle added the extra items to the meat and lowered the flame to let it simmer. Lydia began making a salad to go with their meal. Ladelle started to tell her that he'd make it, but he kept quiet. He went into the bathroom to take a shower but decided to holla at Petie first. That was still his man and he was grateful that Renee didn't run her mouth. Renee called Lydia the whole time he was locked up, threatening her and talking shit. Lydia handled everything like a woman; she never threw anything up in his face about this or that. Renee had come to see him a couple of times, too, threatening him with the bullshit. *This bitch is nuts*, he'd think.

Ladelle was glad when Petie answered the phone instead of Renee. "Yo, what's good, my nigga?" Ladelle said.

"Ain't nothing, dick. I seen Share walking her dog and snuck up on her ass. Yo, La, she looked like she seen a ghost...bitch froze. I started to snatch her up and drag her ass in the house. Her fucking pit saved her bitch ass," Petie said, remembering the look on her

face.

"Why you keep holding on to that shit? Fuck that ho. What's done is done; let that shit ride. You know she a police lover. You better hope she didn't tell them muthafuckas you ran up on her and was harassing her or some shit," Ladelle said, hoping to get through to Petie. They talked for a few minutes more until Lydia called Ladelle to eat. Before hanging up, they made plans to meet up on the weekend and play some ball.

Ladelle took his shower before sitting down with Lydia for dinner. *This is the way shit is supposed to be*, he thought. *Come home from work, eat a meal and lay back with wifey for the night. All that running the streets and shit don't even feel right anymore.*

The pepper steak was good, thanks to Ladelle, but the salad was a little soggy. Ladelle didn't complain. He and Lydia cleared the table, and he washed the dishes while she dried them. She wiped the stove and countertops as Ladelle prepared two bowls of ice cream. Lydia's was strawberry with peanut butter and whipped cream, and Ladelle's was butter almond. Lydia always wanted strange foods now; she ate jelly sandwiches with mayonnaise and pickles with fried eggs, and she would sometimes make pancake mix and add a can of corn to the batter. It was bad enough she couldn't cook, but seeing her eating all this strange stuff was a little overbearing for Ladelle. Lydia would always tell him it wasn't her; it was the baby.

Lydia sat propped up on the couch and Ladelle sat beside her and rubbed her belly, hoping to feel his child move. He was so excited about the baby, and he couldn't wait until he or she was born.

Lydia was even more beautiful to him now; her complexion was like honey, and her hair was thick and down to her shoulders. She had stopped wearing weaves and ponytails and kept her hair braided. She was a shorty—5'1" and 148 pounds. She was thicker now, and Ladelle hoped she wouldn't have any stretch marks.

Ladelle was 5'11" with a stocky build, cut up arms and legs, a six-pack and a chipped tooth, which made his smile unique. His sideburns were trimmed into L's, and he had a thin moustache and grey eyes. Ladelle and Lydia looked like they belonged together.

Lydia graduated college with a degree in marketing while Ladelle was locked up. But she was in no hurry to get back to work until the baby was at least a year old. There was always something on TV about nannies or babysitters abusing children, and she knew she would never leave her child with a stranger; she wouldn't trust anyone with her baby except Ladelle's mother or her sister. But if it came down to her staying home until her child was in school, then so be it.

Chapter Twenty

Venus was trying to calm Share down when Will walked through the door. *Thank God*, she thought. Share was a nervous wreck. She told Venus how Petie had snuck up on her and taunted Pirate. She knew that if Pirate hadn't been with her, he would have done something crazy. Will assured her that everything was going to be all right, but Venus was a little worried because she knew Petie was going to start shit up all over again.

Share went to her bedroom and began to pack some of her clothes. She was going back to her co-op on Seventy-Fourth Street. Fuck that; she wasn't about to live and walk in fear again. She didn't care what Will said; she was outta there.

Will and Kalif were on the phone discussing Petie. "Oh, that nigga is home, huh? Yo, where he restin' at?" Kalif asked.

"I think him and his wife and sons are still on 133rd and Convent, in building 110 on the corner—unless they moved. But I doubt it," Will replied.

Kalif wanted Petie and everybody in his circle dead. He didn't care how many years later it was. He still wanted to put those niggas to rest like they did his brother. And now that Petie was home and showing his face again, it was going to happen.

They decided to pay Petie a visit this week. It was time to get it crumped again, and this time anybody in the way was as good as dead.

Venus looked in the mirror. The plastic surgeon had done an excellent job on her face. You couldn't look at her cheek and tell that at one point it had been stitched up. But every time she thought about Petie, she was reminded of the day Giselle had sliced her.

She continued looking at her reflection and prayed that she wouldn't have to relive the nightmares from three years before; she was getting bad vibes. She knew the look on Will's face earlier was sheer hatred.

Will hated Petie for all the fear he put in Share and for all the hate-mail he'd sent her. Will expected Petie to be a little heartbroken after Share had cut him off, but the cat still had a beef after three fucken years. *Why can't he just get a new shorty?* Will thought.

Venus was certain that Will was going to call BJ and tell him Petie was starting his shit again. She could see why Share wanted to go back to her co-op. She joined Share in her bedroom and helped her pack.

Share drove her Lexus to the co-op and waited for the door-

man to get her bags out of the back seat. She grabbed her coach briefcase and handbag, walked to the bank of elevators and waited. She rode upstairs with another tenant who got off on the fourth floor.

Share walked into her seventh-floor co-op and hit the alarm keypad. She set her things down and went to the bar to make a drink. She called Will to let him know that she was there and would see him in the morning. She wanted to be alone tonight.

Share flipped through the rolodex on the desk in her office and got the number for the District Attorney's office. She was going to call him first thing in the morning. She prayed that Petie would just leave her alone, even though she knew he wouldn't.

It made her laugh when she thought of how crazy he must be about her, as she was with him at one time. *He's whipped*, she thought. She laughed some more until reality set in. No—Petie didn't have feelings for her anymore; he had a score to settle. She was no longer in denial. She knew what time it was. Petie had expressed in all his letters how much he hated her and to not think anything other than that.

Share poured herself another drink and got undressed for bed. She'd be all right after a good night's sleep.

Venus arrived home and as always, the first thing she did was open the back door so Bullet and Diamond could go out back. The place needed to air out. Diamond was pregnant again, and Venus never got the smell out from the last two litters of puppies she had. It smelled like it was *her* place, and Venus and BJ were just visitors.

Speaking of BJ, he wasn't home again. His schedule seemed to change over the past year, and he was hardly ever there. He had one more year of school and he would have his bachelor's in business management. He was going full time and working part time. When he came in, he either had to study or was too tired to spend time with her. They hadn't made love in two weeks and he was always coming in late.

Venus called Share and they spoke briefly. She decided to take Share's advice—strip down, relax and wait for BJ to come home. Maybe she'd get lucky tonight.

"But BJ, why can't you stay just for tonight...p-l-e-e-e-a-se? I'll make sure you're up on time in the morning, and I *might* let you get some sleep," Annette said with his dick between her lips. She sucked hard on the head until she pulled out his cum. Then she looked up at him with her bedroom eyes that always seemed to beg for more.

BJ sat on the edge of the bed and thought about what lie he could tell Venus. He knew she was suspicious because his whole schedule had changed.

"Now, what am I supposed to tell my girl when she asks why I'm not coming in?" BJ asked Annette, knowing that she'd have an answer. He dialed Venus and let the phone ring twice. He hung up before she answered. He knew she couldn't *69 him because Annette had a private phone number. He decided to take his ass home. He would see Annette tomorrow night.

BJ got up to get dressed, but Annette pushed him back

down onto the bed. She got on top of him in the *69* position and went to work on him, and in turn he went to work on her. BJ stuck his tongue in her asshole and sucked her butt juices. Annette hoped not to fart in his mouth.

She told him to wait while she fixed her tongue ring. She bent over sideways and took the phone off the hook. She hit redial and when she heard Venus say "hello," she started calling BJ's name. "Oh, God, BJ, suck it harder. Yeah, baby, like that...ooh, God, I'm cummin'. BJ, suck my juice, daddy, suck it. AAAHHH, yes baby. Now lay back and let me sit on your face," Annette purred, knowing Venus was hearing everything loud and clear. She wanted BJ all to herself and as far as she was concerned, Venus was too old for him anyway. She got up off his face and slowly slid down onto his dick, all the while calling out his name.

BJ, not knowing what Annette had done, said, "You know I love this pussy, right? Damn, mama, fuck your dick, mama...yeah, gimme my pussy, Nette."

After they both came Annette went into the bathroom. She came out quickly and hung up the phone, knowing that Venus had been still listening. She lit a cigarette and lay on the bed. She didn't mind if BJ left now; she knew he'd be back.

Venus was furious. She knew that wasn't somebody playing a joke because she had heard BJ's voice. She now knew why they hadn't been fucking; he was fucking some bitch named Nette. At least that's the name she thought she heard. She had tried to *69 the number, but it was private.

Venus couldn't wait for BJ to come through the door. She

didn't know if she should start packing his clothes or cutting them up. She sat in the living room and waited until she heard the car pull up. She'd been drinking, so BJ had better be ready for a fight.

Bullet went to the door and relaxed when he saw BJ, who came in like he was guilty of nothing. He dropped his backpack and walked toward Venus to kiss her, but she turned her head. "What's good, ma? You in a bad mood?" he asked.

"No. As a matter of fact I'm in a good mood. I just don't like kissing niggas whose breath smell like pussy. Go brush the hairs out your teeth," Venus said getting up off the couch. BJ just stood there looking dumb.

"Did you use a condom? Or do you and *Nette* fuck raw?" she asked him, watching the many expressions on his face. BJ was trying to look confused now. "Answer me, dammit!" she yelled up into his face.

"The fuck you talkin' 'bout, ma?" BJ was wondering how she knew.

"Oh, that's a good one, BJ: The fuck you talkin' 'bout, ma?" she said mimicking him. "Your breath smells like that bitch needs to douche. That's what I'm talkin' 'bout. How's that for starters?!" she hollered before telling him everything she heard through the phone.

When BJ got ready to turn to walk out the door, Venus slapped him like a bitch. He turned around and started choking her. They fell over the coffee table and onto the floor, and he landed on top of her. She dug her nails in his face and scratched him down to his chin. He began to bleed. He got up off of Venus and she jumped up from the floor like a mad woman, tearing at his clothes. She

began to wildly scratch him all over his face and neck now. BJ back-handed her, and her lip started to bleed. She ran into the kitchen and got a pan. She came out and charged at him, screaming. She managed to hit him twice before he tackled her, knocking over the TV. BJ was on top of Venus again, choking the shit out of her, when Bullet locked his teeth around his ankle, tearing through the skin. BJ turned around on the floor and started kicking Bullet with the other foot as he screamed in pain. Venus was trying to catch her breath when Diamond jumped on BJ and locked his wrist between her jaws. BJ was bleeding badly now, with Bullet still tearing at his ankle. It was truly a scene. BJ struggled with both pits, kicking Bullet with his free leg and hitting Diamond with his free arm. When Venus realized that the dogs weren't going to let him go, she called them off of him.

BJ was screaming and crying like a bitch. There was blood everywhere. Venus didn't know what to do first, so she made a drink and sat down.

"What the fuck!" BJ hollered. "Do something! Call an ambulance!"

Venus looked at him like he was Bin Laden. She didn't know who this stranger was in her house. He was a foreigner to her now. "No, fuck that. Tell *Nette* to call an ambulance. And get your chewed-up ass outta my house before I let the dogs loose on you again," she said with a straight face. She felt no mercy—at least not for him. She only felt bad for her dogs because they had blood on them. The only thing she wanted to do right now was give them a bath.... At least *they* were trustworthy. She would take care of them first and then she'd cut up all of BJ's clothes with a box cutter.

BJ wobbled outside, dialed 9-1-1 and waited for an ambulance to come. When it arrived, he told the paramedics he'd been attacked by two pits while walking home from the train station. He would deal with Venus later.

chapter
Twenty-one

Petie was at Fortieth Street waiting to report to his parole officer. He knew his urine was clean, but he hadn't found a job yet. He had been home a little over a month, and his P.O. insisted that he get a job immediately. Petie would try and work around that; this time his P.O. was a woman, and she looked like she hadn't had a good dick in a long time. If push came to shove, he would get at her. But he needed to feel her out some more to see if she was with it. If she was, he'd put something in her back. *She* would be the one looking for a job by the time he was done with her...he'd be the P.O. and she'd be the parolee. The thought made him smile. She called his name and he got up and walked into her office.

She was a little heavy, but she had nice lips. He wondered if she was a head nurse, or in her case the *head* parole officer. He looked at her and wondered how much she weighed...he wouldn't be picking her up. She'd be picking *him* up. She needed to lay off the donuts and leave the corn chips alone. Then maybe she'd slim down.

Petie sat down across from her and gave her his pretty-ass smile. She smiled back. *Yeah, I'ma give big girl something to smile about*, he thought. *She's gonna be one happy bitch*.

Petie got on the expressway and listened to Biggie's *Notorious Thugs* while heading uptown. It felt good to be home. He rode through Washington Heights and hollered at one of his old Dominican connects. He and Calderone talked for a few minutes before coming to an agreement. Calderone knew Petie had just come home, and he remembered the status Petie had before getting knocked. Petie paid him twenty grams and Calderone fronted him ten on GP.

Petie pulled up in front of his building. When he got inside his apartment he put the material in the bedroom. He went back out to the smoke shop and bought a couple of packs of 12 x 12 thins and 12 x 12 regulars to bag up his material. He was ready to jump off again, and the feeling of getting that money made his stomach tighten in knots. He also bought two fifty-cent razors and a pack of Newports and headed back to the crib. He had about eighty dollars in his pocket, and he wanted to set his work on the street quick. Luckily, Renee wasn't home, so he could work in peace. He definitely wanted to be finished before his sons came home. He went to work and after the first forty dimes were ready, he made a phone call.

Ty came through and picked up the first forty from Petie. He left and headed back to his project on St. Nicholas. Ty was nineteen years old now, but Petie remembered when he used to change his diapers. He always thought Ty was his son, because he was fuckng his mother around the time she got pregnant. Ty was a money-gettin' nigga, and he was just fifteen when Petie had first put work in his hand. He proved then that he was about it.

Petie sat back and started making plans for his next move. He was thinking about robbing the Dominicans on Broadway between 139th and 140th Street. Yeah, he would bag them, but right now he wanted to speak to Share.

He called her restaurant on 125th Street and was told that she wasn't in but could be reached at home. Petie didn't have her number; she'd gotten it changed. He found that out when he came home and tried to call her. *No problem, booty-licious; I'll still get at you*, he thought. He missed the way Share sounded when he had his dick in her ass. The thought of her whining voice in his ear made him rise for the occasion.... *Where's Renee?* Petie wanted to be up in something right now. He never had to wait to fuck somebody, especially when he was behind the wall. Mike-Mike was always ready for him with a juice-filled hole. Petie slid up in him easy—no lubrication, no nothing. He thought about the other faggot he used to fuck on a regular while on his third state bid. He wondered where he was now. He would never fuck with either of them in the real world, and he hoped that part of his life never surfaced.

Petie dozed off and was awakened by the phone ringing. It was Ladelle calling to tell him he couldn't see him this weekend because he and Lydia were going to see a play at the Beacon Theater. He told Petie to come by and get him, and they could squeeze in a quick game of basketball. Petie looked at his watch and told Ladelle he'd be there shortly. But first he wanted to check Ty and see what he had for him.

Ty told him he'd given out five sample bags and that he still had about twenty-two dimes left. He had sold thirteen, and Petie told him to sell fifteen more and give him $330.00. He told Ty he'd take care of him on the next pack, and he would. Petie always kept the money black and never shitted on his workers. His word was his bond, and everybody knew that. He stashed the dough and headed to the Polo Grounds to play some ball with the fellas.

Chapter
Twenty-Two

Kalif was leaving the African shop on 125th after getting his braids done over. The girl who normally braided his hair wasn't there, so he had let another chick do it. She was braiding it too damn tight and he told her, "Don't pull my edges. If my hair starts coming out I'm gonna have your ass deported." She assured him that his hair was fine. Kalif didn't like her to begin with. She smelled like rice and old peanut butter. He paid her and bounced.

Will was at the restaurant right across the street. The regular manager, Abdul, was on vacation, so Will was covering for him for two weeks. Kalif entered the restaurant and waited for Will. They left shortly after, hopped in Will's Durango and headed toward Convent Avenue.

Will pulled up in front of Petie's building and he and Kalif got out of the truck. They waited for someone to come out so they could get inside the building. No one did, so Kalif started ringing people's bells. There was a buzz sound, and Kalif stepped in and held the door for Will.

They checked the names and found the apartment they were looking for. "Listen, son. We just comin' to holla at this cat—no drama. Let's see what's good with him and take it from there," Will told Kalif. They rang Petie's doorbell and Renee opened the door. She didn't know who they were and she was a little confused, seeing two young thugs at her door. Kalif asked for Petie and Renee said he wasn't home. She told him to call him on his cell phone.

"Nah, that wont' be necessary," Kalif replied. "What time is he comin' in?"

Renee, sensing that something was wrong with this picture, asked Kalif, "Who should I tell him stopped by?"

Kalif smiled and said, "The boogeyman," and he punched Renee in the face. She fell on the floor and Kalif then kicked her on the side of her head. Darnell looked out from the doorway of his room, saw his mother on the floor and ran to her. Kalif pulled out on him. "Where your old man at, youngster?" Kalif asked him with the heat pointed at his head.

"I-I-I-I don't know," Darnell said.

"The fuck you stuttering for?! What, you a retard or some shit—huh, huh?!" Kalif screamed. Will suggested that they bounce, but Kalif was having fun. And he even thought about taking them hostage to avenge his brother's death.

Renee, in tears, was bleeding from her mouth and ear. Kalif

suddenly hit Darnell with the butt of the gun and bent down and grabbed Renee by the throat before punching her in the face again. Then he did the unspeakable: he pulled out his johnson and peed on her. Will was getting nervous now, and he was ready to leave.

"Tell your husband I'm about to piss all over his world," Kalif said. He shook his dick, put it back inside his pants and zipped them. Will was calling him from down the hallway staircase now. He no longer doubted that Kalif was crazy or had a screw loose somewhere.

Kalif spit in Darnell's face and ran to the stairwell, taking three steps at a time. He got in the Durango and Will dropped him off at Lincoln Projects.

Will tried to act normal when he went back to work. He was hoping that nobody had called the cops. Even though he had maxed out, he still didn't want any contact with the police.

Will called BJ's cell phone to let him know what had just gone down. Venus answered and told him she didn't know where BJ's cheating ass was. She told him what happened the night before and how she had thrown him out. She also explained that BJ's phone had fallen out of his pocket during their fight, which was why she had answered it. Venus told Will that he might find BJ at Lincoln Hospital. And finally, she asked him if he knew Nette. Will lied and said he didn't. He didn't want to be in the middle of that bullshit. He told Venus he'd drop by and pick up BJ's clothes. Venus told him there was no need because she shredded most of his shit and threw the rest of it in the dumpster. She'd take everything that was left and make a bonfire in the backyard with it. Will hung up and called

Lincoln Hospital.

The operator connected Will to BJ's room. BJ told him how he had started to call Venus last night but changed his mind. Annette did some dirty shit with the phone and Venus had heard everything.

"Damn, son. Nette did you grimy, dog. But you dead to the wrong, though. Ain't no way outta that one," Will said, wondering how BJ had gotten caught up with such a grimy chick. BJ told him how Venus had flipped out and attacked him with a frying pan and let the dogs chew him up. They both started laughing, and BJ admitted his defeat.

Will informed BJ what Venus had done with his clothes. "You serious? Yo, what's wrong wit' her?" BJ said. "Yo, she is bugged out. Bullet and Diamond was tearing my shit up, and Venus watched them get at me. Then the bitch got up and made a drink and watched some more. Finally, she called them off of me. Yo, she is fried." Will and BJ continued laughing and joking about what had happened until Will told him he'd see him during visiting hours.

They ended their call, and Will thought about Venus and what she had said to him over the phone. After hearing BJ's version, he was convinced that Venus wasn't fried; she was burnt like toast.

BJ called Annette from the hospital bed and blasted her. She claimed that the phone must have come off the hook and she leaned on the redial button. She swore up and down that she hadn't set him up by calling his house. BJ didn't believe her one bit.

Annette started popping mad shit after BJ told her how

Venus attacked him. BJ wasn't impressed with what she was saying. She sounded corny like cob. She told BJ to come move in with her, and she would take care of him until he could go back to work. *Nah, that is definitely outta the question*, BJ thought. He told Annette he'd call her later and not to call his cell phone because he lost it. *Fuck her*... He wanted to speak to Venus. He wanted to make shit right, but he didn't know where to start.

chapter
Twenty-Three

Petie drove through the streets like a drunk driver, trying to get home. Renee had called and told him that two guys came to the house, pistol whipped Darnell, beat her up and peed on her. Petie was furious. When he and Ladelle reached the front of his building, they saw ambulances parked out front. When they got inside, Renee was describing Kalif and Will to the officers. Her lip and eye were swollen, and the EMTs were trying to get her to go to the hospital. Darnell had a big knot on his head, and he was being taken to Harlem Hospital. Dante was at his aunt's house, and Renee called over there and insisted that he stay put for the weekend.

Petie followed the ambulance to the hospital and Ladelle went to pick up some burners. Whether Ladelle liked it or not, he was back in the game.

When Petie and Ladelle met up again, they drove to Share's brownstone on 142nd and Convent. Petie rang the bell and yelled out her name from the top of the steps, but there was no answer. Pirate could be heard barking from inside the apartment. "I should kill this motherfucka, La," Petie said, ready to put a bullet through the window of the door and shoot Share's pit.

"We'll come back later. The bitch ain't home," La said. They hopped in the Navigator and Petie headed back to Harlem Hospital.

Darnell was conscious. Petie looked down at his son and became enraged. His sons were all that mattered in his life. Niggas violated by going to his house and getting his family involved.

Darnell said he knew one of the cats. He told Petie he recognized him as the manager of the McDonald's on 125th and Eighth. Darnell said he had stopped there after school a couple of times. Right away Petie knew who he was talking about—Share's man. Darnell went on to describe Will's appearance, and Petie remembered him clearly. When he began to describe Kalif, this time Ladelle knew who he was talking about. He told Petie how he and Biz had caught Kalif on Edgecomb Avenue. They talked about Kalif being Rasheed's younger brother, and how he was on a rampage to avenge his death. Petie didn't give a fuck about Rasheed, Kalif or any of those muthafuckas. He was ready to catch two bodies and add two more teardrops to the three already under his left eye.

Petie and Ladelle pulled up in front of Petie's building and parked the Navigator. Petie ran inside and got two ski masks and strapped a burner to his waist. They went outside and caught a cab to the 125th Street McDonald's.

Ladelle paid the cab and Petie went inside the restaurant. He waited in line and eyed all the male employees working there. No one fit the description that Darnell had given him. He was about to leave when Will came out from the back, carrying a cash register. He then opened the drawer of the register for one of the cashiers. Petie checked the name plate on his chest—it was Will.

It all made sense to him now. Petie remembered that night he answered Share's phone and the caller had said his name was Will. Yeah, that was the same cat from the bank. He looked a little older now, but it was him.

Petie went back outside and told Ladelle that he had seen Will. He told him to stop a cab and wait across the street for him, and he walked back into the restaurant, wearing his ski mask and waving his gun.

When Petie got back to his apartment, he threw the ski mask and clothes that he had worn down the incinerator. He was glad that Renee was at her sister Rhonda's house with Dante for the weekend. But he was angry that Will had gotten away. He couldn't believe that he had missed that nigga. He figured the police were all over the restaurant by now, so there was no going back. He put on a fresh pair of jeans and kicks and headed back to the hospital to see Darnell.

Ladelle had bounced on Petie. Fuck that; he wasn't about to get caught up in a Mickey D's shootout. He could just see all the news channels reporting that shit. No, he didn't want any part of that.

He called Petie on his cell phone. He lied and said he had to bounce because Lydia was having pains in her stomach.

"How the fuck you gonna bounce and leave me solo, dick?!" Petie shouted angrily.

"Yo, what the fuck you wanted me to do? I thought Lydia was having the baby?" Ladelle yelled back.

"Having the baby? Having the fucking baby! She's six months, nigga! How the fuck could she be having the baby?! You left me solo—type of shit is that? Listen, I'm at the hospital and I'm going to see my son—one." Petie clicked off the phone and registered at the front desk.

Ladelle felt bad, but fuck that; he had too much to lose. He was about to parole out of work release in six more weeks, and he had just made his board, so he didn't care what the situation was; he wasn't going to lose his date due to some dumb shit. Granted, what those niggas did to Renee and Darnell was foul. But if Petie hadn't fucked with Share again, they wouldn't have even known he was home. As far as Ladelle was concerned, this wasn't his beef. Besides, he had a baby on the way and too much to lose. Let Petie shoot shit up by himself.

Chapter Twenty-Four

Kalif and LeRoy were outside St. Nicholas projects waiting to see a couple of chicks. Kalif told LeRoy that if either of them was ugly, he was going to chase her down the expressway in the Range Rover. They both laughed and continued to wait on the chicks.

Ty came out the building and said, "What's up?" to them and kept it moving. They all knew each other and there was no bad blood between any of them.

As Kalif told LeRoy about the episode hours earlier at Petie's house, somebody yelled out the window to Ty, telling him he'd left his cell phone upstairs and that Petie had called. Kalif looked up at the window and then over at Ty, who was now walking back toward the building. Kalif almost couldn't believe that this could be the same Petie cat. There was no way.

Ty got to the building and waited to be buzzed in, and Kalif walked in behind him and caught the door before it closed. He stood behind Ty, thinking about how he was going to take him.

"Yo, you know Petie from 133rd?" Kalif asked him.

"Yeah, that's my man. He on his way here to pick up something now," Ty answered, not knowing he was about to die.

"Thank you, partner," Kalif said before yoking Ty up, dragging him over to the stairwell and shooting him twice in the head. He then emptied his pockets and walked out of the building. He told LeRoy he had to bounce and would see him later. LeRoy had no idea what was going on, and he went on waiting for the chicks without Kalif.

Petie pulled up minutes later and beeped his horn. He hollered up to Ty's window, and someone hollered back that Ty came in the building but maybe stopped on the third floor at his girl's house.

Petie pressed the buzzer and waited. LeRoy stood there listening, wondering what was going on. *First Ty went inside the building and never made it upstairs, and then Kalif bounced...and what's taking those chicken heads so long?* he thought.

LeRoy recognized Petie, but he just didn't know where from. *Who is it?* he heard a female voice say through the intercom.

"Denise, it's Petie. Yo, tell Ty to come down," Petie replied. Denise said Ty wasn't there, and he should buzz him upstairs at his own apartment. When LeRoy had heard Petie say his name, he tried hard to remember who he was.

Petie was starting to think that Ty had stepped off on him.

Once again he yelled up to Ty's window for somebody to let him inside the building. The buzz sounded and he pushed the door open and walked to the elevator. After waiting impatiently for a few moments, he decided to take the stairs.

Petie opened the stairwell door and saw a pool of blood. He looked behind the staircase and discovered Ty's body. He threw up and ran out of the building. He buzzed Denise again and told her to call an ambulance.

LeRoy was talking to the girls who had finally made it down-stairs. They all watched as Petie ran to his ride and sped off like a roach running from Black Flag. One of the girls opened the front door of the project with her key, and the three of them went inside the building. Petie's bloody footprints led them right to the staircase entrance.

"Oh shit!" LeRoy said when they pushed open the stairwell door. The girls began to scream, and they ran out of the building. Denise came outside and one of the girls took her to the staircase. She broke down, crying and screaming.

The lobby got crowded, but there was still no ambulance. LeRoy decided that it was time for him to bounce; if an ambulance ever did arrive, the police would be on the scene, too. Besides, he wasn't trying to hang around and politic with muthafuckas. He jumped in his Range and was ghost.

LeRoy called Kalif, and before he could ask him if he had shot Ty, Kalif said, "So did that nigga Petie show up at the projects? I left him a surprise in the building, ya heard?" Kalif began to laugh at what he had done, and he seemed proud of it. LeRoy told him how

Ty's girlfriend and the two chicks they'd been waiting on had started screaming, and he decided to leave shortly afterward.

LeRoy was becoming more and more leery of Kalif. He still hadn't gotten over Rasheed's death and everybody knew it. But to think he was going to be running around killing niggas on G.P. made LeRoy want to stay away from him. A nigga like Kalif would have everybody doing twenty-five to life.

"Nah, I can't see all this drama, son. I'ma holla at you later," LeRoy said. He clicked off his cell and headed home... *Yeah, my nigga, I'll see you later—like some time next year. You a little too loose for me right now*, LeRoy thought. He suddenly remembered the name *Petie*. It all came back to him; they had a shootout with his mans uptown. Those cats killed Rasheed, and then one of them shot a cop. *That's who Petie is*. No, he didn't want the business. He didn't want any part of that shit.

Kalif sat in his livingroom smoking a blunt laced with dust and drinking Henney. He thought about his next move. Who would be his next victim?

Kalif was soon fucked up and he began to hear voices. Every time he heard the elevator stop on his floor, he thought someone was coming through the walls. He took the pistol from under the sofa and cocked it. He walked through the apartment, pointing the gun in various directions. The dust had him toasted.

All of a sudden he felt somebody walking on his heels. He turned around and waved his pistol, trying to hit whoever or whatever might be there. He went into the bathroom and pulled back the shower curtain. It looked to him as if someone had just gotten out of the shower.

Kalif heard his cell phone ringing in the living room. He tried to go and answer it, but his feet were sinking in the carpet. *What the fuck is happening? Niggas put quicksand in my apartment!*

The phone stopped ringing. Kalif was crawling on the living room floor when Fluffy, his cat, came and rubbed up against him. He grabbed the cat and tossed him out of the window like a paper towel. "Oh, shit! What the fuck was that?!" somebody yelled from outside.

Kalif was tripping even more now from the dust. He opened his apartment door, looked down the hallway and saw figures coming at him. He slammed his apartment door and went back inside, but the figures had followed him. No, they weren't figures; they were...*what the fuck?!* Kalif's mind was racing. "Oh, God, it looks like snakes!" he screamed. "What the fuck is that?!! Kalif began shooting at the snakes in the apartment. He scrambled to his feet and ran back to the door. He ran out of the apartment in his boxers and a T-shirt. He was wearing one Timberland boot and was still holding the gun in his hand. He yelled all through the hallway, banging on people's doors with the butt of the gun.

The entire hallway was filled with snakes, and they were coming toward him. "AAAAAHH, somebody help me! Open the fuck-en door!" Kalif screamed like a lunatic. He'd never had a bad trip like the one he was having tonight.

Kalif made it downstairs and saw some of his neighbors

huddled together on the main floor. *What the fuck is wrong with him?* they all thought when they saw him. He ran out of the building thinking the same thing about them, not understanding why they weren't trying to get away from the snakes. "Quicksand, watch your step!" he yelled out frantically in front of the building.

Derek and Freestyle were out there now, and when they saw Kalif running around in his boxers and a T-shirt with one boot on, they knew he was having a bad trip. Derek walked over to Kalif and tried talking to him in an easy tone. He was nervous because Kalif still had the gun in his hand. "Yo, Kalif, put the gun down, man. Ain't no snakes out here and ain't no quicksand in the hood. And be easy with that heat in your hand, dog."

One of the neighbors came up behind Kalif and grabbed him, and Derek and Freestyle took the pistol from him. The hood knew Kalif smoked dust and spazzed out from time to time, but this episode was the worst.

The man who had grabbed Kalif was like an uncle to all of them. He'd know what to do once they got Kalif up to his place.

Kalif was born and raised in Lincoln Projects, and everyone who lived there knew that he hadn't played with a full deck since he was a kid. But now, since his brother had gotten killed, he really was out there. It was like his elevator went up but never came back down, or like his telephone was always out of order. He just wasn't right.

Derek knew Kalif had to stay out of his own apartment. It seemed haunted by his mother's death, and now Rasheed's. And every time he smoked that dust, those demons came to life.

Chapter
Twenty-Five

Share was talking to the detectives at her restaurant. Will had called and told her what had happened. He assured her that none of the employees were physically harmed, but they were all shook up after the ordeal.

The police began marking shell casings from the bullets that had been fired. The video camera located at the front of the store had been shot at and stopped recording. Fortunately, the other camera had captured footage of all the activities of the day. The detectives were viewing that tape on a VCR that was used to train new employees. There on the screen was Petie when he first entered the restaurant. He left and returned, wearing a ski mask and shooting his way through the building. The tape was put in slow motion so the detectives could get a good look at him. They also tried to identify

Petie's accomplice outside the store at the time of the shooting. Finally, they began to interview the customers and employees.

The detectives had everything they needed to make an arrest. Share filled them in on the letters that Petie had sent her prior to his release. She told them everything she knew, including his address and his friends' names, and she prayed that they would catch him. After she told them about Petie's history and the case that he was still on parole for, they were anxious to arrest him. Petie was bad news, and his rap sheet had violent acts that he'd committed listed all over it. One of the detectives asked Will if he knew why this 'Petie guy' would be trying to kill him. Will didn't offer any information. He just told them "No."

Petie rode down St. Nicholas Avenue to 125th Street. He wanted to ride past McDonald's and see what it looked like. There were police everywhere, and undercovers were all over the place. He saw Share's car, and Will was standing outside talking to the detectives. "Police-lovin' muthafuckas," he said aloud. He headed home, but as soon as he drove up Convent Avenue he saw a blue and white outside his building, along with some plain-clothes officers. Petie panicked. He pulled over and parked, turned off the ignition and watched them. They rang the intercom and somebody buzzed them in; he knew it wasn't Renee because she was at her sister's house.

The officers came back out after what seemed like forever. Now they appeared to be just hanging around. Petie started the Navigator, made a quick U-turn and headed to the Polo Grounds.

He grabbed his cell phone and called Ladelle. Lydia answered the phone and told him he wasn't home. She said she didn't know where he was and that he was probably in the Bronx. Ladelle was sitting right there listening. He had told Lydia what to say. He didn't want to be bothered; Petie wasn't trying to change. Nigga wanted to keep doing the same thing over and over. Ladelle wasn't feeling that shit anymore. He gave Lydia a signal to hang up the phone. Petie started telling her how the police were looking for him and that he was going to Queens for a couple of days. He told her to have Ladelle call him in Queensbridge. He knew the number out there.

Lydia hung up the phone and told Ladelle that they should have their number changed; she didn't want Petie calling anymore. He was bad news.

Ladelle told her he was going to holla at Petie on some serious shit. He hadn't told her about the McDonald's episode. He knew she'd break, and he didn't want her stressing and possibly complicate her pregnancy. Ladelle loved Petie in his own way, but he knew he was going to have to cut him off. It was just one of those things.

Petie decided that it was now time to finally get even with Share. He would fuck her before going to Queens...*bitch wanna talk to the police and lay me down again*, he thought before parking in front of her brownstone. He didn't see her car anywhere and she didn't know what he was driving, so the element of surprise would be perfect.

Share left the restaurant and decided to shop on 142nd Street. She wanted to feed Pirate and take him for a walk when she got home. The detectives had said they'd notify her when Petie was in custody, and they asked Will to go to the precinct and give a state-

ment. They believed he knew what had prompted the shooting. They thought it was over drug money and didn't believe Will when he'd said he didn't know what was going on.

Share turned on her block and parked. She sat in the car for a few minutes, trying to digest all the events of the day. She got out and took her Coach briefcase from off the back seat. She then hit the car alarm and took her house keys out of her purse. Petie eased up behind her as she put the key in the lock. "Open the door and put the dog away before I kill both of y'all," he said and placed his burner firmly to the back of her rib cage. The only thing she could do was obey.

They stepped inside the foyer and into the hallway of the brownstone. Pirate came running down the steps and Share instructed him to go back. He did what he was told. Share locked him in one of the rooms and turned toward Petie. "Now what?" she said. He back-slapped her without hesitating. Share fell hard to the floor and looked up at Petie with a bloody lip as she tried to crawl away from him. He took off his jacket and reached down and popped the chain that hung from her neck.

"Petie, please, I never did anything to you. Just tell me what you want, and I'll give it to you now. I swear I will," Share cried, with blood spilling from her mouth and snot dripping out of her nose.

"Take off your clothes before I rip them off," Petie ordered. Before Share could move, he pulled her up off the floor by her throat. Petie ripped the clothes from her body and dragged her into the bedroom by her hair. Share began to scream.

"Stop fucken screamin' and cryin'. You wanna make all that

noise—huh? I'm gonna give you reason to make noise," Petie said. He spit a razor out of his mouth and cut off Share's bra and thong. She stood before him, naked and shaking. She had never been so scared in her life. Petie asked her whether she was going to give it to him or did he have to take it.

"Fuck you!" Share said and spit in his face. Petie wiped her saliva from his face with his finger and licked it. "You sick son of bitch. I don't know how I could ha—"

Petie punched her in the face before she could finish her sentence. He unzipped his pants and pulled his dick through the zipper hole. He pushed Share onto the bed and lay on top of her with his dick and knees in her face. He was shoving his meat into her mouth when she bit him. Petie hit Share in the face until she stopped moving. He went to the dresser and pulled two pairs of pantyhose out of one of the drawers. He pulled Share up to the headboard and tied each of her arms to the bedpost with the pantyhose. She lay on her stomach now, and Petie got completely undressed and lay back on top of her, rubbing his dick between her butt cheeks. She pleaded with him to stop, but he ignored her and roughly entered her. She was bleeding when he finally pulled out; he had ripped her. He rammed his dick back into her ass and fucked her over and over.

Share went into shock and somehow shitted on herself. Petie got up and walked to the bathroom sink, washed the blood and feces off his dick and left her lying there.

Will came in the house and called out to Share. There was no

answer, and he thought she might be asleep. But Pirate was barking like somebody had snatched his food. He let Pirate out of the room, and he frantically rushed past Will and ran up the steps.

Will called out to Share again, and Pirate was barking like a mad dog now. Following Pirate, he walked to the top of the stairs and saw Share's clothes thrown about. He walked into the bedroom and stopped in his tracks. Share was tied to the bed, and blood and shit were all over her legs. The room smelled like raw ass.

Will ran over to the bed and untied Share. He called 9-1-1 and then he called Kalif. Petie was definitely going to die tonight.

Chapter
Twenty-Six

Venus was recuperating from a hangover. She hadn't been to work and she hadn't heard from BJ. She decided to call the hospital and get his room number. Her head pounded when she moved, and she felt like she had to throw up. Venus started drinking again, knowing full well that she was an alcoholic and should stay away from liquor.

The phone rang. It was Will, calling to tell her that Share was in the hospital. Will told her everything, from the incident at McDonald's to coming home and finding Share. Venus was in shock. She hung up, washed her face and drove to Columbia Presbyterian.

Share was lying on her side when Venus arrived. There was a cop outside the hospital door. Venus knew it was serious now, seeing

Share with police protection. *Why did she ever get involved with Petie to begin with?*

Share smiled up at Venus, who bent down and kissed her forehead. "How are you, sissy," Venus asked her with tears in her eyes.

"I'm in pain and I can't shit. The doctors want to give me a bag to shit in," Share said crying. "He ripped me up bad, Venus, and I have internal injuries...he fucked up my insides." Venus wiped Share's tears and then wiped her own. Share's face was beat up and her lip had four stitches in it.

Venus wanted to kill Petie. Share told her the doctors were running lots of tests on her—including the one for HIV. Petie had ripped her so badly that the doctors had to give her eleven stitches to close up the wound. She said it hurt even when she peed.

Venus and Share talked until the nurse came to give Share a shot of morphine. Venus watched as her best friend dozed off into a restless sleep.

She quietly left the room and approached the officer outside the door. "Please make sure that anyone who comes to see her shows proper identification...please, sir," she begged. "Guard her with your life." The officer told Venus that he would do his best for the eight hours he was there.

Venus left and headed to Lincoln Hospital to see BJ. Now that her mind was clear, she would listen to what he had to say.

Will and Kalif were sitting in the Durango when Ladelle and Lydia pulled up in front of them. Ladelle was getting a bag of groceries out of the car and Lydia was walking toward the building. Kalif recognized Ladelle immediately. "Yeah, that's one of the niggas who jumped out that burgundy truck on me—him and this other cat. This Jamacian kid tripped me up, and that's how they caught me. But that's definitely him," he said.

Ladelle didn't notice them at all. And he had no idea what was about to go down.

BJ was ready to leave the hospital. He felt handicapped. There was a cast on his ankle and his wrist was bandaged up. Being that he worked at Lincoln Hospital doing custodial maintenance, the entire staff knew him. There were flowers and cards all over his room, but enough was enough; it was time to go.

BJ was sitting up in bed eating fruit when Venus came through the door. Damn, he loved her. She stood there looking at him for a few moments and finally said, "Do you mind if I come in? Don't worry; I left the dogs home." BJ smiled at her and they both started laughing. Venus sat on the side of the bed and kissed him. "I'm so, so sorry, baby. I swear I am. I was just so hurt, hearing you over the phone with that...girl." She didn't know what to call Annette.

BJ came clean with her about everything and hoped that she would take him back. She told BJ she didn't know if she could ever trust him again. After speaking further and going back and forth, they finally decided to start over.

Venus told BJ about what had happened to Share and the

condition she was in. It had been one thing after another lately.

Venus left the hospital and went to the ATM to withdraw some money. She then filled up her gas tank and went shopping. She wanted to replace some of BJ's clothes that she'd cut up. Afterward she went to Pathmark to buy groceries.

BJ would be home tomorrow. He said he'd be leaving with or without the doctor's consent. Venus knew she couldn't stop loving him just like that. And she didn't want to anyway.

Renee was on the phone talking to Petie. She told him his picture was on the news and he was wanted for attempted murder, rape, assault and a bunch of other charges. Petie told her to go home in the morning, gather up some of his clothes and meet him in Queens. Renee wanted to know what he'd done. "I'll explain everything later, ma. I love you, and tell my sons that Daddy loves them to death," he said brushing her off. Renee hung up wondering what he had gotten himself into now.

Renee wanted to call Ladelle. He had been acting real shitty towards her since he came home, and especially since Lydia was pregnant now. *How could he forget all the times we spent together—all the freaky things we did? Don't I mean anything to him? Apparently not.*

Renee wanted to fight Lydia again. *That bitch can't even fight*, she thought. *Punk bitch.* She decided to wait until Lydia had her baby and then catch her ass outside the projects and put the beats on her—embarrass her right in her own hood. *Why not? It'll give the neighbors something to talk about.*

Petie was at Roz's house in Queensbridge. She was a chick he used to fuck with. He needed to hide out for a minute. NYPD had put out an all points bulletin for his arrest. The news reporter had said that he was armed and dangerous, and no one other than the authorities should try to apprehend him. Instead, the public was urged to call 9-1-1 or Crime Stoppers.

Roz was a bonafide thoroughbred. He knew she would let him lay low. He was thinking about going out to Pennsylvania, and from there down south. He didn't really have a plan, but he wasn't going to let anyone take him alive. He wasn't trying to go up North on rape and sodomy charges. *Fuck it*, he thought. *I'ma shoot it out with them niggas. Fuck them charges and the police...live by the gun, die by the bullet.*

Chapter
Twenty-seven

Share's doctor came into her room, and she knew something was wrong by the look on his face. He told her that the internal bleeding had stopped. That was the good news. The bad news was that her HIV test came back positive.

"Noooo!! Oh, God, please...no! Doctor, please tell me there's been a mistake. Please, doctor. Oh, God, retest me, please," Share pleaded, unable to accept what the doctor had just told her. He said that if she wanted to be re-tested, he'd arrange to have her blood work done again.

Share lay in her hospital bed and cried until her head hurt. There were so many things going on in her mind. *Did I get infected when Petie raped me? Did Will infect me? How am I going to tell Will? Should I even tell him? Are people gonna look at me and know*

I'm HIV positive? How am I gonna live with a death sentence? Should I tell Venus? How is she gonna react when I tell her?

Share's pillow was soaking wet from her tears. She felt sorry for herself. Her face was battered, her ass was sewn up...and the doctor said she was HIV positive. How could all this be happening to her? She was a businesswoman, damnit, and these kinds of things didn't happen to women like her—but they *did*.

Share thought about a way to get to Petie. The answer came in an instant. She could talk to Renee. She knew Renee, but Renee didn't know her. Well, after she got finished talking to her, she'd know everything about her.

Share called Venus and told her the news about her health. They both cried, and Share told Venus that she was planning to call Renee. Venus said she would make the call for her and bring Renee to the hospital. She knew it was the only way Share could get some answers. She just hoped it wouldn't make matters worse. Share gave Venus the number as they prepared to hang up.

Renee picked Darnell up from the hospital and took him to her sister Rhonda's house. She had a lot of running around to do. She called Ladelle and he asked if he could meet her over at her building. He wanted to give her something for Petie.

Ladelle was sitting outside when she got to the front of her building. He opened the window and gave her a thousand dollars. He told her to take care and he pulled off. That was it; he had nothing else to say to her. Renee was disgusted. *Fuck you*, she thought.

Dick was corny anyway. He had a nice tongue game, but that was about it. Besides, he made more noise than I did. Fuck him!

Renee went upstairs to her apartment and got some clothes together for her fugitive husband. She gathered clothes for the boys, too. She didn't want them back in the house until those two thugs were caught.

Renee checked her answering machine. She knew everyone who called except for one person. She played it again and heard Venus' voice, asking her to please call her. It concerned her husband's health, and maybe hers, too. *What the fuck is that about?* she thought.

Renee immediately called Venus back. She listened in horror as Venus told her some of what she knew. Renee wanted to meet Share. She wanted to see her face-to-face.

Petie was laying up with Roz in Queens. He hadn't fucked with her in a while, and she took it in the ass, too. *Nasty bitch*, he thought. He also thought about how he had rammed Share in the ass and she shit on him. That's what saved her. If she hadn't done that foul shit, he would have still been up in her.

Petie called Renee at her sister Rhonda's house and was told that she had to make a run. He left word for her to call as soon as she got in. She never did.

Renee got to the hospital and waited for Venus. Venus had told her what she looked like and what she'd be wearing. Renee thought it was some kind of setup at first, but her heart told her it wasn't.

Venus arrived late and apologized. She and Renee introduced themselves to each other and registered for Share's room. Renee did not know that Share's boyfriend was one of the guys who had come to her apartment that day, and she didn't know about Share's involvement with her husband. Renee also didn't know that Petie had infected Share; Venus only told her that he had raped and beat her so badly that she had to be hospitalized. Venus told Renee that there was something else she needed to know, but she had to hear it from Share.

Venus and Renee walked into Share's room. Venus immediately walked over to Share, who was lying on her side, and hugged her. Share introduced herself to Renee and started off by saying, "First off all, I'm sorry that I had to meet you under these circumstances. Unfortunately, certain events have occurred that left me no choice but to speak with you." Renee looked at her and thought about how professional she seemed. Share told her about her and Petie's relationship—how it started, the times they spent together and how often. She also informed Renee how he flipped when she told him not to call her anymore, and how she had shot Giselle in self defense. She told her about everything that went down, except how Will and the fellas had jumped Petie and put him in the hospital.

Renee was numb when Share was done. There was nothing she could say. Then finally, Share told her about her HIV test, and Renee broke down in tears. Seeing her cry made Share cry. They

talked some more and Renee told Share she would turn Petie over to the police herself. She wasn't only hurt, but she felt embarrassed, knowing that Petie had brutalized a woman like that. She knew he was violent, and she told Share she believed everything she had said.

Renee bent down and hugged Share. Now she wanted answers from Petie, and after she got them she was going to tell the police of his whereabouts.

Renee was devastated. When she left the hospital she didn't go back to Rhonda's house; she went to the Department of Health and took an HIV test. She wanted the results right then and there. God forbid she was positive, because if she was she was going to beat Petie with a golf club. But first she'd make Jell-O out of his balls. Yeah, Petie was a dead man if she was positive. He wouldn't have to worry about the police, because she'd kill him.

She thought about all the times she and Ladelle were together and didn't use protection. *What if we both have it? Would that mean Lydia and the baby have it too?* Lots of people's lives were at stake now because of her no good, low-down, cheating-ass husband.... *If Petie did give the virus to Share, then where did he get it from?* Renee knew he wasn't gay, but she wondered about his activities during the times he was locked up. There was too much going on. She needed to sit back and just breathe.

Chapter Twenty-Eight

Petie was on his way back to Manhattan. Ladelle had agreed to meet him at Copeland's on 145th. Renee never showed up with the money or his clothes... *What the fuck happened to her? And why is Ladelle acting* so *funny all of a sudden?* Petie was suspect; he didn't really trust anyone now that there was a manhunt going on for his capture.

Petie pulled in front of Copeland's Restaurant and waited for Ladelle. After a few minutes passed, he got out of his truck, went to a bodega and bought a beer and a pack of cigarettes. On his way back he saw a kid he knew named Bobby who he'd been locked up with while on his second state bid. Bobby had lost a lot of weight. He looked like he was smoked out or sick, one or the other. Petie got back in the Navigator and talked to Bobby from the window.

"So what you been up to? Look like you shed some pounds," Petie said to him.

"Yeah, I lost a little weight," Bobby replied. He was dressed in a Sean John suit and a pair of Kenneth Coles.

"So, what—you smokin' on the down low or what?" Petie asked him, thinking he already knew the answer.

"No, I don't fuck with that shit. I got the virus," Bobby told Petie and saw the expression on his face immediately change.

"Oh, shit!" was all Petie could say. He told Bobby to take care of himself and he kindly dismissed him. Petie wondered how long Bobby had been sick. He should have asked him. He used to run up in Bobby when they were in the same housing unit. Damn, now he had something else to worry about.

Ladelle pulled up and parked behind Petie. He opened the passenger side door of the Navigator to get in and he and Petie sat and talked for a few minutes. Ladelle said he couldn't understand why Renee hadn't met up with Petie, because he'd given her the money hours ago. Petie thought that maybe the police were harassing her, thinking she knew where he was. That was the only reason he could think of that would keep her from contacting him. Ladelle told Petie he loved him like a brother, but he was done with all the rah-rah shit; it was over for him. He said the only things guaranteed from that lifestyle were prison and death. It was time for a change. Ladelle and Petie gave each other a firm hug, and Ladelle headed home where he felt he needed to be—with wifey.

Petie took a chance and went to his house. Fuck it, he had to. Renee had disappeared and he needed to get some things from the crib anyway. He rode around and made sure that the coast was clear. Finally he made it inside the apartment and got the rest of the work he had stashed. Petie grabbed the bags, the scale and threw some clothes in a backpack. He hit *69 on the phone to see who had called the house last. After hearing his cell number, he pressed *play* on the answering machine and skimmed through the messages that Renee had already heard but never erased. When he heard Venus' voice he wondered, *What the fuck did she call here for?* He was sure it was some catty shit Share had put her up to, and he went on to the next message. He didn't have time for the bullshit right now. He bounced and headed back to Queeens.

Kalif was in the bathroom washing himself off. When he was done he went into the living room and gave Des two dimes for the head job, but she wanted more. "If it wasn't for me, you wouldn't even know where Ladelle lived, nigga—not to mention that I *can* give you his exact apartment number. Hit me off for that information, Kalif. You know I always come through for you," she said shoving the two dimes inside her bra.

"What's the apartment number?" Kalif asked her. She told him and he threw her two more dimes. "Now beat it," he said. Des knew how Kalif was, so she bounced.

She remembered when she and Petie used to cut up bricks in her house, bag them up and get money. Des had let Ladelle and Petie keep work at her crib all the time. Then she started smoking. She had lost her apartment and was in the street turning tricks now.

When she heard about Rasheed's death and Petie and Ladelle being connected to it, she started giving Kalif information about Ladelle and pumping him for crack. Des didn't know what Kalif was going to do, but she knew it was on and poppin'.

She stashed the two additional dimes and went back out on the street in search of another dick to suck. This time she needed money. She didn't have anywhere to go and she needed some quick cash for a cheap hotel room; she was tired. She was thinking about going to the rehab when some cat said, "Miss, you wanna hang out?"

"Yeah, where we goin'?" she asked.

"To my crib. I got a room on 128th and Park." Des was straight for the night.

Chapter
Twenty-Nine

Venus and BJ pulled up in front of their apartment. BJ was on crutch-es, and Venus grabbed his backpack and held the door open for him. The minute they got inside, Bullet and Diamond started growl-ing and barking at BJ. Venus had to put the pits away just so he could come into the apartment. She helped him into the bedroom and then went to check her messages.

BJ's cell phone was on the nightstand by the bed. He picked it up and checked all the missed calls he had. They were all from Annette and he immediately erased them. He hopped into the living room, leaving the crutches behind and sat on the sofa. There was a faint spot on the carpet where he had bled that Venus tried to clean. It reminded him of the night they fought. It was their first fight. It upset him to think that he had gotten physical with Venus in that sort of

way. He remembered when his father used to beat his mother, and he had vowed to never hit a woman. If anything, he should have hit Annette. *Grimy bitch*, he thought. To think she had been blowing up his phone. *What if Venus had answered?* But it didn't make a difference now anyway, because he had already come clean with her.

Venus had fried fish because she knew it was BJ's favorite meal. They ate and watched a DVD afterward. When the movie was over, they turned on the news. *If anyone has seen this man...*the reporter stated, and a photo of Petie flashed across the screen. She recapped the vicious attack on Share and the attempted murder of Will at McDonald's.

Venus and BJ sat in silence as they listened to the story. The reporter urged viewers to call Crime Stoppers if they had any information on Petie's whereabouts. He was a wanted man.

Good for his ass, Venus thought. She turned off the TV and she and BJ got ready for bed. She thought about the fight they had the last time they'd been home together. *I guess that makes the relationship official*. She began to laugh. BJ asked her what was so funny. "It's just one of them things," Venus said.

What the fuck is wrong with everybody? Petie wondered looking at his phone. It seemed as if everyone was turning their backs on him. *Fuck it*. He got undressed and went into the bedroom to bone Roz. *She* wasn't turning her back on him, and if she did, it was only because she wanted something up in her.

Petie lay there after they finished fucking and smoked a cigarette. He fell into a nightmarish sleep. He dreamed about the police kicking in Roz's door and shooting up the place. If it had to come down to that, then that's just the way it would have to be.

Chapter Thirty

Ladelle was up bright and early for work. Lydia was still in bed, so he made a bowl of Apple Jacks and a glass of orange juice. He knew she'd be home all day and he wanted to come in early so that they could go to a movie. He went into the bedroom and bent down and kissed her on the forehead. "I'll see you when I get in tonight," he said before walking out the door.

Ladelle didn't wait for the elevator; instead he took the stairs down, two steps at a time. He passed by some chick on a lower floor taking a hit, blowing the smoke down the stairwell. "Get the fuck outta this building with that shit!" he barked at her.

Ladelle walked through the lobby, exited the building and went to a newsstand. He grabbed the Daily News and a pack of gum. He took out the keys to his Escalade and stopped dead in his tracks before hitting the alarm on the key ring. He dropped the newspaper and walked over to where his ride was parked. "What the fuck happened?" he asked out loud. It was obvious what had happened; somebody had trashed his ride.

Ladelle couldn't believe his eyes. All of his windows were smashed out, someone had slashed his tires with an ice pick and there was spray paint all over the sides of the truck. The seats, dashboard and roof were all cut up, and there was more spray paint throughout the interior.

Ladelle was tight. There was no way this was his ride. He called 9-1-1 from his cell phone and then he called Lydia upstairs.

The police arrived and Ladelle gave them a full report of what had happened to his truck. Lydia had come downstairs by the time he was done. Ladelle called his insurance company and then he called AAA. When they arrived, Ladelle filled out the necessary paperwork and showed his title and registration, along with his license to prove ownership of the truck. They surveyed the damage and towed the Escalade away. It was a good thing he had full coverage or he'd be fucked.

Ladelle walked Lydia back to their building and caught a cab to midtown. He was already late, and he knew that traffic would be a monster now. *Better late than never*, he thought.

Lydia got upstairs and made some tea with milk and honey. She was worried about Ladelle. She wondered if maybe she'd made a mistake in marrying him. Now someone had taken their anger out on his Escalade. Somebody was definitely sending him a message. But she knew it came from his dealings with Petie. Lydia wanted

Petie out of Ladelle's life once and for all. All he did was bring trouble to people. He destroyed lives and she didn't want Ladelle to have anything to do with him anymore.

Lydia called her girlfriend, Janine, and told her that she was coming over. She didn't want to be in the house alone, and she needed someone to talk to.

Kalif was having breakfast at Pan Pan's on 135th. He called Will to find out how Share was doing. Will told him she was all right and would be home from the hospital next week. He was going to stop in at the McDonald's restaurant on Fordham Road for a couple of hours before going to see her.

Kalif and Will talked about BJ and his fight with the dogs and the foul shit Annette did. Kalif told Will he used to fuck with Annette and that she was mad grimy.

They ended their call, and Kalif went back to Lincoln and rolled up a blunt. He called Carlito, his Latino dust connect, and made arrangements to see him on 141st and Seventh at Drew Hamilton Projects. No sense in having the trees without the dust. That would be like having chicken without any seasoning or pancakes without the syrup as far as he was concerned.

The weather was good, so Kalif jumped on his mountain bike and rode to Drew Hamilton. He stopped on the way and hollered at a chick standing in front of a corner store. He told her to watch his bike, and he went inside the store and bought two more blunts and a pack of Certs; her breath smelled like a sour mop. Kalif came out of the store and gave her the pack of Certs. "Here, ma. Suck on them real slow, okay? After you freshen up, I'll holla at you," he said.

"Fuck you, nigga! You ain't all that!" she said as Kalif got back on his bike.

"Yeah, aiight, but at least my breath don't smell like a hall-way," Kalif replied. He rode his bike in traffic until he got to Drew Hamilton. He saw Carlito—a Puerto Rican kid—and got two bags of dust from him. Kalif wondered where this nigga copped from. Every time he asked, Carlito acted liked it was some ancient Chinese secret, so he just stopped asking.

Carlito had some Dominican chick with him. Kalif winked his eye at her. She smiled and winked back. *No good bitch*, he thought. *Here she is with this cuchifrito and winking at me*. He thought about hitting her doggy style. Shit, if he did that she'd tell him where all the stash spots were. And by the time he was done with her, she'd be bringing him bricks that *she* had stolen—anything for the anaconda.

Kalif wondered what her tonsils felt like. She looked like she had a deep throat. He got back on the bike and before pulling off, he beckoned her to him. She moved closer to the bike, smiling and lick-ing her lips. Kalif turned and farted, and then he took off. She was one of those *now & later* bitches: *I'll hit you now and dis you later*.

Kalif got back to Lincoln and grabbed his blunt. He dropped one of the bags of dust in it and fired it up. He took a few pulls and began to feel lifted. He walked to the kitchen and opened a beer before returning to the living room to watch rap videos on BET. When

Kalif went back to the kitchen to get another beer, he saw somebody standing in the hallway. He blinked his eyes and looked again, and he saw a male figure standing there laughing at him. Kalif walked toward it, but it disappeared. He went to his bedroom to look for the figure. He looked under the bed and in the closet...there it was, still laughing at him. Kalif went to grab at it, but it went through the wall into the bathroom. *What the fuck is happening?* he thought. Kalif ran into the bathroom and didn't see anybody. He was totally tripping. He opened the medicine cabinet and closed it back. Then he turned on the sink faucet and leaned forward to splash water on his face. After drying off his face he looked in the mirror and saw someone standing behind him. Kalif turned around and saw no one. When he looked back in the mirror he saw his reflection melting. He tried to grab at his skin to keep it from slipping off his face, but it continued to melt. His face was falling apart. "Oh, God, what the fuck is happening?!" he yelled at his reflection after seeing his nose fall off and his eyelids slide down the drain.

Kalif ran out of the bathroom and stood in the living room with his back to the wall. His skin started to crawl and his head began to itch. *Oh, no*, he thought. *Ants are on me.* He looked down at his feet and saw about a million ants beginning to crawl up his body. Kalif got the broom and started swatting at them. They were all over him now, including his hair. He shook his legs frantically and beat himself in the head, trying to get the ants out of his hair. They wouldn't budge.

Kalif ran back into the bathroom, turned on the shower and got in the tub fully clothed. He let the water pound down on him and finally washed away the invisible ants.

Kalif got out of the tub and took off his clothes. He dropped them in a pile on the floor and stood in the bathroom butt naked. He didn't want to look in the mirror; he didn't know what he'd find there looking back at him. His earlier reflection had scared him to death.

He went to his room and got in the bed underneath the covers. He grabbed the gun that was under his pillow in case the figure reappeared. He would shoot it if it did. Kalif lay there in bed naked for hours, waiting for the figure to return. He saw nothing, but he did hear something—the voice of Rasheed, his brother who was taken away from him by knuckleheads. He missed him so much and his heart was in pain.

Kalif knew what he had to do to let Rasheed rest. He had to bury the niggas who had killed him. They wanted beef, well, they were gonna get it.

chapter
Thirty-one

Lydia was spending the day with her girlfriend, Janine. She needed to clear her mind and get her thoughts together. Janine had four kids, and Lydia was attached to the youngest—thirteen-month-old Janelle. Janelle would start to cry every time Lydia would get ready to leave, so Lydia suggested that she keep Janelle overnight. Janine was more than happy to have one less child to clean up after, so Lydia made Janelle an overnight bag and put her favorite teddy bear in her pocketbook. She called a cab and headed home with Janelle.

The cab pulled up to Lydia's building. She sat outside with Janelle for a little while and then pulled out her keys. She took Janelle by the hand, put her overnight bag over her shoulder and walked toward the building's entrance. A guy approaching from behind asked her to hold the door for him. She held it without a second thought. The guy was Kalif.

Lydia pressed the elevator button and waited. The elevator doors opened and Lydia, Janelle and Kalif, who was listening to a set of headphones now, all got on it. Lydia pressed *14* and Kalif pressed *12* as the doors closed. When the doors opened back up on the twelfth floor, Kalif got off and told Lydia to take care. She told him to do the same, and the elevator doors closed again.

Lydia exited the elevator when it got to her floor. She had the key in the door when Kalif walked up on her. She panicked when she saw the gun in his hand.

"Open the door, prego, before I drop this rug-rat down the incinerator," Kalif said to her as he snatched Janelle up in his arms. "What an ugly little girl. The doctor should have slapped your parents," he added looking at Janelle.

Lydia opened the apartment door and Kalif stepped in behind her and closed it. He took the keys out of her hand and put them in his pocket. He put Janelle down and took the keys out of his pocket after realizing that a key had to be used to lock and unlock the door, even from the inside. This was even better than he had expected. He locked the door and put the key back in his pocket.

"Who are you?" Lydia asked, reaching for Janelle. She wanted to keep her from crying, even though she felt like crying herself. Kalif told her his name was *The Coroner*, and that's what she should call him. Lydia looked at the blank expression on his face, and it dawned on her who he probably was. She wanted to ask him about the Escalade, but there really was no reason to; she knew he was responsible.

"Please, this is my girlfriend's daughter and I'm pregnant. Please don't hurt us," she pleaded.

"Oh, this is your peep's daughter? Well, that bitch needs to go to prison for endangering the welfare of pretty muthafuckas like me," he said with no feeling at all.

Janelle began to cry and Lydia tried to comfort her, but it wasn't working. "Please, she's just a little girl, and you talking like that is scaring her."

"Scaring *her*? Scaring *her*?! You can't be serious. She's scaring *me*, with that ugly face of hers, now shut the fuck up!" he shouted, still wearing the same blank expression.

Kalif asked Lydia when Ladelle was coming home. She started to say any minute, hoping that would scare him and make him leave, but she changed her mind and said she didn't know. He told her that the sooner she found out, the sooner he'd be leaving. Suddenly, he looked at her and started laughing. Lydia asked him what he was laughing at. "I'm laughing at you," he said. "Now stop asking me questions."

Lydia noticed that Kalif had an odd look on his face now, and she asked him what he planned on doing. He looked at her and said if she asked him one more question, he was going to put Janelle in the freezer.

Lydia viewed him as a little boy who didn't get enough attention during his childhood. And she could tell by the blank look in his eyes that he was a couple of sandwiches short of a picnic. She wondered if he was a maniac, but she decided that he looked too young to be one. She was wrong.

Kalif told Lydia to get some rope. When she told him she didn't have any, he went to her bedroom in the back, looked through the dresser drawers and found a pair of pantyhose, using them to tie her hands behind her back. Janelle started crying again and Lydia tried to comfort her, but there wasn't much she could do now with her hands bound. Kalif yelled at Janelle to stop crying, and that made her cry even more. He told Lydia he'd put her in the closet if she didn't shut up.

"Please untie me so I can feed her, and then I'll try to put her to sleep," she pleaded, hoping he would feel some kind of sympathy. He agreed to untie her, but only because Janelle's crying was getting on his nerves.

"If you try anything funny, I'll push you out the fucken window. I'm not playing, so don't sleep on me," Kalif said as he untied Lydia's wrists. He went on to tell her that the two most important things in his life were money and drugs, and he didn't give a fuck about her. He also told her that his mother and brother were both dead, so dying meant nothing to him. That alone told Lydia that he didn't care about her life or the baby she was carrying.

Lydia was trapped in the house with a nut and had no idea what time Ladelle would be coming home. She couldn't help but wonder whether Kalif would let her go or really hang around until he arrived. And when he *did* get home, what would Kalif do then? In the meantime, she was stuck in the crib with a nut and didn't know if she was going to live or die. She couldn't bear the thought of what the end result might be.

Chapter
Thirty-Two

Lydia put Janelle to sleep and laid her down in the spare bedroom. Kalif tied her hands back up again and ordered her to sit on the living room couch. He sat across from her at the dining room table and began to roll a blunt with the bag of dust he had left. Lydia asked him again what he planned on doing. "Kill your man," Kalif said flatly. "Then I'm going home to watch a movie. Now don't ask me no more questions." Lydia wondered if there was any way that she could somehow notify the police, Ladelle or Janine.

"I'm having some discomfort sitting like this with my hands behind my back. It's putting too much pressure on the baby. Can you please untie me? I'm not gonna try anything. I swear," Lydia said. Kalif looked at her and thought about it. He put down his blunt and ordered her over to him. She did as she was told. He untied her hands and went back to rolling his blunt.

"Where's the bathroom?" Kalif asked.

"Down the hall on your left," Lydia replied, pointing in the direction of the bathroom. Kalif picked up his blunt and walked to the bathroom, and Lydia rushed to the phone and dialed 9-1-1.

Hello, 9-1-1, what is your emergency?

"A man is holding me hostage at 2991 Eighth Avenue— hurry," she whispered into the phone.

I'm sorry, ma'am, please speak up. What is your emergency? the operator asked again, already putting a trace on the call.

"2991 Eighth Avenue—14C," Lydia quickly said and hung up the phone before sitting back down on the couch.

Kalif flushed the toilet in the bathroom. He came back into the living room and looked at Lydia through dust-filled eyes. She didn't look right to him. He asked her to stand up and turn around. Then he told her to sit back down before going to the kitchen and getting a beer out of the refrigerator. He came back and sat down at the table again, eyeing Lydia carefully and suspiciously. He was about to have another trip.

Kalif looked at Lydia and wondered what was wrong with her head. Her hair was styled in a French twist, with Shirley Temple curls around the back and front. Kalif tilted his head and looked at her stomach now. *What the fuck is going on?* he thought. *Why is her stomach so fucken big? Oh, God! Her hands look like claws!* Kalif thought about Freddie Krueger and decided to tie that ass up again. It was the only way he could be safe; she wasn't going to cut him up with those claws.

Kalif grabbed the pantyhose from off the floor, and this time he tied Lydia's hands over her stomach where he could see them. He backed away from her and rubbed his eyes, still wondering what was wrong with her head. Then he studied her face and wondered, *Damn! Is she cock-eyed? Why she keep lookin' at me?* Kalif decided that he would have to fix that. He went back into the bedroom and took the pillowcase off of a pillow. He returned to the living room and put it over Lydia's head. She began to cry, and she pleaded with him to not hurt her or the baby.

Kalif mistook her crying for laughter and after a few moments, he was convinced that she was indeed laughing. Enough was enough. He went to the bedroom once again, and he took a pair of socks out of the dresser drawer. He came back into the living room and snatched the pillowcase off Lydia's head. He shoved the socks in her mouth and put the pillowcase back on her.

Officers from the 32nd precinct had been dispatched to Lydia's apartment. The operator reported her call as suspicious because she had hung up before identifying herself. But it was still being treated as an emergency and not a prank.

The police arrived at Lydia's building and rang her buzzer three times. Kalif sat there looking at the house phone like he had never seen one before. Lydia knew, of course, that someone was ringing to gain access to her apartment and the phone wasn't ringing. *Thank God*, she thought. She tried to talk, hoping that Kalif would take the sock out of her mouth.

He walked over to the couch and snatched the pillowcase off her head. Lydia looked up at him with tears in her eyes. Kalif couldn't believe what he was seeing. Her eyes were leaking. "Yo, what are you?! Why your eyes leakin'?! Turn them off!!" Kalif was yelling like a madman. Lydia continued to cry. She had tried to be brave, but it wasn't easy with this lunatic screaming at her. Kalif yelled again for her to turn off her eyes. Lydia was now totally convinced that he was insane.

Kalif took the sock out of her mouth and threw it on the floor. He marched away from her like she was his arch enemy, and the look on his face was one of sheer horror. There was snot coming out of her nose now, and her eyes were red from crying.

"Aaaaaahh!! What the fuck are you?!" Kalif screamed when he saw the snot dripping down her chin, and he accused her of having worms. Lydia had no idea what he was going to do next. His back was up against the wall now, and if it wasn't for the sheetrock, he probably would have gone through it.

Lydia made an attempt to get up off the couch, thinking she might be able to talk to him in a way he'd understand. Kalif pulled out his burner and said, "Back up, alien! I seen your last movie; I know how you disguise yourself. B-a-a-a-ck up!" he screamed. Lydia sat back down, wondering where the hell the police were. Kalif started asking her a bunch of weird questions like, "How long you been on this planet?" and "How did you get here?" There was no reply. "Answer me, you freakazoid!" he shrieked.

Lydia burst into tears, which only made matters worse. She didn't know what to say to Kalif. All she could think about was that she was going to die at his hands and never get the opportunity to give birth.

Kalif now stood with his back and the bottom of his right elevated foot against the living room wall. His burner rested on his knee, and it looked like he was posing for a picture as he kept his eyes on Lydia. As far as he was concerned, something might jump out of her stomach and onto his face. He wasn't as stupid as she might think. He had seen *Aliens*—part one *and* two.... *She has the nerve to look scared—ha! The nerve of her*, he thought. Of all the chicks to take hostage, he had to pick an alien. The dust really had him zoning.

The doorbell rang, and Kalif jumped up off the wall and stood erect. He put his index finger to his mouth, signaling for Lydia to be quiet. He thought more aliens were coming, and he tiptoed toward the door.

"Police! Anybody in there?!" the officers yelled from the hallway. Lydia wanted to scream out, but the only thing stopping her was knowing she might be putting Janelle, who was still asleep in the spare bedroom located way in the back, in harm's way.

The officers called out again. "Police, open the door!" Kalif froze like an icicle.

"Help, he's got a gun!" Lydia yelled, not knowing where she got the courage to do so.

Kalif walked over to her and smacked her off the sofa. She hit the floor hard. He put the burner to her head and looked at the door. "I'll kill this bitch right now! Get the fuck out of here! I'm not playing!" he screamed.

"Please, he's got a gun to my head! Oh, God, please, do what he says or he'll kill me and my baby!" Lydia cried out. The officers at the door immediately called for assistance. They had a hostage situation going on and they didn't want to be responsible if anything went wrong.

When the Chief of Police arrived, he instructed his officers to evacuate the fourteenth floor and the two floors above and below it. He called the precinct to get the phone number in the apartment so contact could be made. Meanwhile, Eighth Avenue was swarming with emergency response vehicles, the Hostage Rescue Team and the SWAT team.

The senior negotiator was able to make contact with Kalif. He asked him what his demands were. Kalif didn't have any demands. He told him he wanted Ladelle dead. The negotiator had no idea what Kalif was talking about. Before he could ask any more questions, Kalif said, "I'll let you speak to the alien, but not now." He hung up and fixed a blank stare on Lydia.

The negotiator became a little confused when Kalif referred to Lydia as an alien. He knew Kalif didn't know what he was doing and this wouldn't likely end with anyone being hurt, which was always the best case scenario. He had handled a number of hostage takings in his career, and all of them ended with the hostages being released unharmed. He didn't have any background information on Kalif, but after talking to him briefly over the phone he wondered if he had a mental history. He was more than qualified to handle this, but it would help if he had something to go on.

The negotiator called Kalif back and requested to speak with Lydia. He had to make sure she was alive before taking things any further. Kalif untied her hands and gave her the phone.

"Are you okay?" the negotiator asked Lydia.

"Yes, I'm just scared," she replied with Kalif sitting across from her, watching her like she was a thief.

"Is he alone?"

"Yes."

Before Lydia could say anything else, Kalif snatched the phone out of her hand. He put the receiver to his mouth and said, "If you'd like to make a call, please hang up and try your call again." He slammed the phone down and lit a cigarette, blowing the smoke in Lydia's face.

"What do you plan on doing now?" she asked Kalif.

"You'll know when I do it—now be quiet."

Lydia was trapped in her own apartment with a nigga who didn't care about dying. She did the only thing she *could* do. She prayed.

Chapter
Thirty-Four

Venus had already left for work by the time BJ woke up. She left him a plate of French toast in the microwave. He was a little leery about being in the house alone with the dogs; Bullet and Diamond kept following him around like he was going to steal something.

BJ sat on the sofa and reached for the remote control when he heard his cell phone ringing in the bedroom. He hopped to the room and looked at the caller ID. It was Annette. He wanted to speak to her to tell her to stop calling him. He hit the *yes* button on the phone. "Why haven't you called me?" Annette said before he could say hello.

"I thought I told you when I was in the hospital not to call me anymore. I told you I don't want to be bothered," he said thinking about how much he hated the sound of her voice now.

"Oh, you back at that bitch's house and now you don't want to be bothered? How could you be there, after what she tried to do? She was gonna let them dogs kill you, or did you forget that quick?" BJ hung up on her. Two seconds later the phone rang again, and before he could cuss her out she said, "I'm pregnant." BJ froze. That was the last thing he wanted to hear from her. It had to be a setup.

"How I know you pregnant by *me*? Matter of fact, I don't even want to hear that dumb shit, Annette. Just leave me the fuck alone, you heard?"

"Please, just come over so we can talk like mature adults," Annette said. BJ agreed to see her, but he wanted to get it over with so he could be back home by the time Venus came in from work.

When he got to Annette's house, she was waiting for him in the bedroom—naked. "Get dressed," he told her, walking out of the bedroom.

"Why? You might get tempted to cheat on your old girlfriend again?" Annette said, following him down the hallway and rubbing her titties.

"Don't flatter yourself. Get dressed or I'm out," BJ said without turning to look at her.

They were in the living room now, and Annette was wearing a thong and a pair of heels that didn't look right to BJ. Nothing about her looked right to him anymore. She sat with her legs open on the armrest of the sofa, straddling it. BJ wasn't impressed. Annette arched her back and leaned forward to kiss him, but he backed away and sat down in the corner love seat. She looked like a snake in heels to him.

"Listen, enough with all this bullshit. How do I know you're pregnant by *me*? What, you think I'm gonna believe you just because you said so?" BJ said.

Annette was shell shocked. She couldn't believe her tactics weren't working. "You're the only one I ever fucked without a condom," she said trying to sound convincing.

"Yeah, right. Check this out: I was born *at* night—not *last* night, so tell that bullshit to a newborn," BJ said getting up to leave. He told her he wanted no parts of her, and she began to flip out. This was truly a kick in the face. "The only baby's mother I'll ever have is Venus, you heard?" BJ added. He grabbed his crutches and headed for the door.

"Fuck that!" Annette screamed, running out of the living room behind him. "Who the fuck you think you talking to?"

"Get out my face, Nette," BJ warned.

"Make me!" she screamed again, snatching his crutches from underneath his arms. BJ lost his balance and fell against the hallway wall. Annette was standing in his way now, blocking his path so he couldn't leave.

"Get out the way. Why you acting like a little girl?" BJ said. "You knew about wifey to begin with, and now you talking this pregnant shit. Get out my fucken way!" Annette pulled and grabbed at his clothes, still trying to prevent him from leaving. He shoved her aside and opened her door as she stood there crying.

"Get out!" Annette shouted, pushing him again. Instead of hitting her, BJ kept it moving. Annette ran outside after him and pushed him once again. He tripped and fell down the last few steps,

landing on his back. He didn't move. Annette, scared now, ran down the rest of the steps and kneeled over him, calling his name—nothing. She called it again...nothing. Annette panicked. She tried to get him up off the ground. His body was heavy in her arms. She felt his neck for a pulse, and it was then that she realized he was dead.

Annette ran back up the steps and called 9-1-1. She lived in a private house, and she didn't realize that her landlady, who lived on the first floor, was home and had heard everything. While Annette was waiting for the ambulance to come, so was she.

When the police arrived, Annette told them that BJ had slipped on his crutches and fell. She said when she opened the door she saw him lying at the bottom of the steps. She was crying hysterically and they appeared to believe her story.

The ambulance arrived and rushed BJ to the hospital. After being pronounced dead, his body was turned over to the coroner.

BJ's aunt called Venus at work and told her about his death. She told her the same thing the police had said: BJ slipped and fell after leaving Annette's house. The first thing Venus wanted to know was who the hell was Annette, and what was he doing at her house. BJ's aunt told Venus that the girl was taken into custody, but they hadn't charged her with anything.

Venus was a wreck. She couldn't believe that BJ was dead. She wanted to talk to this Annette girl and find out what her relationship was to him. And she prayed that Annette wasn't who she thought she was, even though her gut had already told her.

Share was watching television in her hospital room when Venus called and told her what had happened to BJ. Share looked over at Will, unsure of how to tell him that his best friend was dead. *If it ain't one thing it's another*, she thought.

"Don't play like that, ma," Will said to her when she finally told him about BJ.

"I wish I was," she said. Will got up and grabbed his coat, kissed her on the forehead and bounced. He had to get some air; the room had suddenly seemed to be closing in on him. He headed to Annette's house with the quickness.

When Will arrived at Annette's house she was drinking, and the air smelled like she had just finished blowing trees. He asked her what happened.

"So it was an accident?" Will said after hearing her story. Annette nodded her head yes. "But you did push him?" he added.

"Yeah, but I was only trying to get him to stay and listen to me," she said trying to sound like the victim. She thought about how she had tried to run that pregnant shit on Will, too, once, but he didn't go for it.

Will wasn't feeling Annette at all. He already knew he was going right to the precinct to tell the cops what she had just said. *Fuck that. You're not gonna kill my peeps and get away with it*, he thought.

It seemed that everything was happening all at once: first, Share telling him that she was positive, and now his best friend was dead. Will had to be strong for Share, and for himself as well.

The officers at the precinct were more than interested in

what Will had to say. They already had their suspicions about Annette anyway, and now they were confirmed. Will gave a written statement of everything Annette had told him. The officers said they'd follow up with him on his account of what happened and pay Annette another visit.

Will left the precinct and headed back to the hospital. His plate was full and he didn't know how much more he could take.

Will called Venus and let her know that he had spoken to Annette. He said she told him what really went down.

"So, that bitch killed him?" Venus said, on the verge of flipping out.

"Yeah, but she made it seem like it was an accident. She said BJ went to leave and she tried to stop him. He turned around like he was going to hit her and she pushed him away from her."

"Yeah, right. That bitch pushed him because he probably told her he didn't want to be bothered anymore. Where that bitch live at, Will?"

"Don't worry about that. I already went to the precinct and talked to the police. I told them everything she said. They're gonna get her. Just be easy," Will said, hoping that would calm her down. It did. He told her the most important thing right now was making funeral arrangements for BJ—first things first.

The officers returned to Annette's house to question her, but she wasn't home. Her landlady invited them inside the house, and they asked her if she had seen or heard anything that day.

"Well, I heard the boy tell her it was over between them. He said he didn't want to be bothered, and she started screaming and hollering. The next thing I know, the door opened and the boy was telling her to get out of his face. Then I heard him fall," she told them as she sat holding a handkerchief in her hand. A little dog lay at her feet. He looked as old as she did.

"After the fall, what did you hear?" one of the officers asked. He was wondering how good her memory was; she appeared to be more than credible.

"Well, the next thing I heard was Annette going down the steps. She must have stopped when she got to the bottom, because the next thing I heard was her going back up the steps."

"Ma'am, why didn't you say anything before about this?"

"Because nobody asked me," she replied flatly.

The police waited outside in their car for a few minutes for Annette to come home. When she didn't, they left and returned with a warrant for her arrest.

When Annette finally arrived home, she was greeted by the police and homicide detectives and was served with the arrest warrant. She put up a fight before being handcuffed, and she was also now being charged with assaulting an officer and resisting arrest. She was making matters even worse for herself, as if she didn't already have enough problems.

After being fingerprinted at the precinct, Annette was allowed to use the phone to make her one call. She contacted her mother and told her what happened.

What?! The police are charging you with killing BJ?! Are they

crazy?! What precinct are you at? her mother shouted at the other end of the line.

"Mom, just go to the courthouse in the Bronx; that's where I'll see the judge," Annette said. She was then told by an officer that she had to hang up. She did as she was told and was escorted back to her holding cell.

The next day Annette's mother posted her bail of fifteen thousand dollars. She was released.

Chapter
Thirty-one

The police were able to contact Ladelle at the midtown restaurant where he worked. He was frantic when he found out what had happened to Lydia.

He ran out of the restaurant to the street to hail a cab. He couldn't believe that Lydia was being held hostage in their apartment. Ladelle knew this was all connected to Petie and his Escalade getting trashed. He was going to cut Petie off for sure now. The shit had gone too far.

When Ladelle got uptown, the police weren't letting anyone enter the building. He identified himself and was put in a van with the hostage negotiator. Janine was also in the van being comforted by crisis workers. She was a wreck over her baby girl, Janelle.

News vans were everywhere, and a crowd of eager reporters had

their cameras rolling to get the breaking story.

The negotiator was asking Ladelle all kind of questions abut Lydia and their relationship as if he had something to do with the situation. This shit made him even madder than he already was. He told them that Lydia was pregnant and about what had happened to his truck, which he filed a report on. He also revealed what he knew about Kalif and that he might think he had something to do with his brother's death a few years ago. Ladelle didn't care that he was possibly giving the police something else to look into; he just wanted Lydia safely out of their apartment. The information helped the negotiator build a psychological profile on Kalif to go along with the arrest record he already had on him. He was very professional, and Ladelle felt that he was going to do his best to get Lydia out of this mess as quickly as possible.

Hours had passed, and the surrounding floors had been evacuated and security was tight. However, Kalif still hadn't made any demands. The negotiator contacted him again and asked him what it was that he wanted.

"Get me some food and some icecream," Kalif demanded.

"Okay. Whatever you want, we'll get it. But you gotta understand that we can't help you if any of the hostages are harmed. Do you understand that, Mr. Reynolds?" the negotiator asked Kalif.

"Oh, y'all muthafuckas know my name?" he said and then paused for a moment. "Listen, I understand. You just make sure I get what I want and nobody will get hurt in here—ya heard?"

"I hear you. Now what exactly would you like for us to get you to eat?"

"Get me some beef and broccoli and some butter pecan icecream. And make sure it ain't melted. I want a pack of Newport 100s and get me two phillies. You got that?" The negotiator repeated Kalif's order and told him they would get it right away.

The Hostage Rescue Team had set up an ambush outside for Kalif. They would make their move when his food was delivered. The SWAT team had already entered the building. A helicopter flew above the location, and the pilot landed the aircraft on the side of the building in a spot where he thought Kalif wouldn't recognize it. Meanwhile, the SWAT team was entering the apartment across the hall from where Lydia lived.

Kalif looked out of the window and saw the helicopter. He grabbed Janelle, now awake, out of Lydia's arms and held the scared child out of the window, dangling her like a doll. Lydia screamed for him to stop before he dropped her. Janelle was crying and trembling now, and Kalif kept her hanging while law enforcement watched in terror through their binoculars. The helicopter circled back around the building, and Kalif pulled Janelle back inside and threw her at Lydia.

The phone rang and Kalif immediately answered it. It was the negotiator. "Hey, if you pull anymore stunts like that, you're going to leave us no choice but to start applying force. We're doing everything you ask us to do, but if you continue to behave recklessly you're going to make us change our plans. I thought we had an agreement that nobody would get hurt."

"Yeah, whatever," Kalif said. "Now let me tell you something: if I see another fucken helicopter out there, I'll drop this rug-rat out

the window. Do you understand that? You talkin' 'bout reckless...y'all keep playing with me and I'll show you reckless. Now, where's my fucken food at?!" he yelled into the phone as Lydia looked at him in complete horror.

Members of the Emergency Response Unit and the Hostage Rescue Team, along with other law enforcement agencies, were all inside the building now. They had entered through the back way. The entire area was closed off to the public, and the reporters and their news vans were still on the scene, catching everything live.

Kalif turned on the TV and wasn't surprised to see his picture on the screen, along with footage of him holding Janelle out the window. "Shut her up before I drown her ass in the toilet," Kalif shouted when Janelle started crying again. "I'm trying to watch the news!" Lydia held Janelle closer to her and began to sing gently. She wasn't putting anything past Kalif; there was no telling what he might do after seeing him hang Janelle out the window. Kalif told Lydia that Denzel didn't have anything on him right now; after seeing himself on all the news channels he felt like a star.

The phone rang. It was Ladelle. To his surprise, Kalif gave Lydia the phone. He figured that Kalif didn't know who he was.

Ladelle didn't waste any time. "Listen to me, and don't show any emotional reaction to what I'm about to say. The building is swarming with police. They are right across the hall. When he opens the door for his food, run in one of the bedrooms and lock the door. You hear me?"

"Yes, the baby is fine," Lydia said pretending to be engaged in small talk with Ladelle.

"Is he right there?" Ladelle asked her.

"Yes, I'm hungry," Lydia said continuing with the small talk.

"Okay, baby, hang up. And remember what I said," Ladelle stated.

"I'll let you go as soon as I eat and kill your man.... The next time they call I'm gonna tell them to send your bitch-ass nigga up here, and you and the little girl can bounce—fair enough?" Kalif said to Lydia as she hung up the phone. Lydia shook her head yes.

The doorbell rang and an officer outside in the hallway called out to Kalif, telling him that his food had arrived. "Leave it at the door!" Kalif yelled back to him. He listened until he heard the officer leave, and then he slowly opened the door with the burner in his hand. Before he could bend down to pick up the bag, the door across the hallway was flung open and there were six guns pointing at his face.

"Drop your goddamn gun, asshole!! Now!! Drop it!!" the SWAT team screamed at him.

Ride or die, Kalif thought, and he licked off two shots before being tackled to the hallway floor. He was then thrown up against the wall and back onto the floor before being handcuffed. One of the officers kicked him and another one spit on him as he was being restrained.

Lydia and Janelle were rushed out of the apartment and were escorted onto the elevator. When they got outside, a huge crowd of people began to clap and cheer, glad to see that they had made it out alive. They were put in one of the police vans as Kalif was being brought out of the building in handcuffs.

Kalif was greeted by the same crowd of people who had just clapped and cheered for Lydia and Janelle. They were now angry. They began to throw bottles at him, and someone grabbed at his shirt. He was eventually bum-rushed and thrown to the ground, and several police officers watched in amusement as he was kicked and beaten.

Kalif was badly bruised when the police picked him up off the ground. They took him to an ambulance where he was strapped down onto a stretcher. The angry crowd refused to let the ambulance move. More than eighty people blocked the vehicle. "Let him die!! Let him die!!" they shouted. One of the officers picked up a bull horn and addressed the crowd, finally persuading them to let the ambulance move. Kalif was taken to Harlem Hospital, where he was arraigned on several charges.

chapter Thirty-Five

Lydia and Janelle were taken to the hospital to be treated for trauma. Janine was glad to have her baby girl back safely.

Ladelle held Lydia in his arms like she would disappear if he let her go. "Did he put his hands on you in any kind of way?" he asked her.

"He hit me once, and he tied me up and put socks in my mouth," she replied.

"I swear to God, if I get my hands on that nigga, I'ma kill his ass," Ladelle said.

"I think he was smoking some stuff, because the house smelled funny when he came out the bathroom. Then he just started to act real different," Lydia said.

"What—he was smoking trees or something?" Ladelle

asked, wondering what she could be talking about.

"I don't know—something I never smelled before." Lydia continued to tell Ladelle how Kalif just started tripping, and talking about aliens and worms.

After being examined Lydia was released. The doctor had told her to go to her regular physician for a follow-up.

Lydia was shaken up and didn't want to stay in the apartment. Ladelle took her to his mother's house for the night.

The Hostage Rescue Team had agreed to meet with Lydia in the morning so she could make a statement. She wasn't ready to deal with all of that, but she knew she had to so Kalif couldn't walk the streets anymore.

Ladelle went back to their apartment and put some clothes and personal items in a bag for Lydia. He went to his stash spot and took out some money. The last thing he wanted was for the police to find it and start asking a bunch of questions. He called Lydia at his mother's house. He told her that he was on his way back over there, and he asked her if she needed anything else.

"No, just get here," she said. Ladelle told her the authorities were still at the apartment and they couldn't stay there if they wanted to. They'd be there until further notice.

Ladelle just wanted to take a shower and go to sleep. He prayed that tomorrow would be a better day.

A week later, Will and BJ's aunt were making arrangements for his wake at Convent Baptist Church on 145th Street and Convent

Avenue. The church was packed with all of BJ's co-workers, family, his peeps from the hood and some of his old college classmates. Venus knew the majority of the people in attendance, but she didn't know how loved BJ was until now. It made her cry even more. Almost everyone he'd come in contact with in his twenty-six years had come to pay their respects. BJ didn't have a large family, but his street fam came from as far as Georgia and Virginia to lay their brother to rest.

The preacher gave a beautiful sermon that put everybody in tears. Some people spoke about BJ when he was younger and how good he was on the basketball court as a kid growing up. Will spoke about how BJ had turned his life around after coming back from up North. He had been determined to do the right thing and never look back. That made Venus cry even more; she remembered how motivated BJ was when he started going to college.

When BJ's aunt began to sing *Black Butterfly*, the whole church was in tears. She sang the song even better than Deniece Williams did. Everyone shed tears for their brother, who had passed away before his time.

A female in a black dress approached BJ's casket as his aunt continued to sing. "Oh, God!" she screamed, as the tears began to roll down her face.

Venus wondered who she was. "Who is that?" she asked turning to Will.

"Nobody. Believe me, she's a nobody," he replied, hoping that Venus would be satisfied with his answer. She wasn't.

"Will, don't lie to me at a time like this. Tell me who she is,"

Venus insisted. Will looked at her and contemplated on it. He finally told her that the crying woman was Annette.

"What the hell is *she* doing here?!" Venus said furiously. She told Will to get her out of there immediately. Will just looked straight ahead, ignoring her request.

When the song was over, several people got up to take one last look at BJ. Annette was still standing at his casket when Venus walked up to her and said, "You don't belong here. Leave now." Annette's tears stopped in an instant. She turned them off like a faucet. Venus told Annette who she was and then told her to bounce.

Annette spazzed out. "Oh, so you're the old lady he was messin' with?" Venus took a step back and started to size up Annette. "Did he tell you I was having his baby?" she added. "Oh, I guess not! He always talked shit about you anyway—especially that you were seven years older than him...now I see why he was always at my house—look at you!"

By now there was a crowd of people staring at Venus, who had said nothing to defend herself. But when Annette started to sound off again, she grabbed her with the quickness and threw her to the floor. She jumped on her and pounded her like a nail in the wall. Venus got to her feet and pulled Annette up off the floor, punching her and knocking her into two other mourners. She grabbed Annette's hair with one hand, and with the other hand she uppercut her in the ribs. A group of people had to tear Venus off of Annette, who continued on with her tirade until Venus told everybody that she was out on bail for BJ's death. That's when everybody went ballistic, pushing Annette out the door. "Get the fuck outta here!" they all shouted.

Annette hopped down the stairs with one shoe in her hand. She looked like she had been ambushed. Venus stood at the entrance just staring at her. She was ready to jump on her again.

Everyone was ushered back inside the funeral home. Venus addressed the other mourners, apologizing for the disturbance. Will got up and hugged her, and she began to cry in his arms as everybody prepared to go to the gravesite at Woodlawn Cemetery.

Chapter Thirty-Six

Renee was at the clinic waiting to get her results from the HIV test. The counselor entered the waiting area and motioned for her to come into her office. Renee was nervous; she'd never had an HIV test before, and the anticipation over the past two weeks had almost killed her.

The counselor asked her what she knew about HIV. "Not that much. Please just give me my results," Renee said.

"You realize that a positive result doesn't mean you're going to die. There are many—"

"Listen, just give me my results," Renee said cutting her off. The counselor took the paper containing Renee's results out of a folder. She looked at them, placed them on the desk and sat back and folded her hands. Then after a few seconds she removed her glasses before looking across the desk at Renee.

"Your test came back reactive, which is a positive result for the HIV virus. Now, what I would—"

Renee jumped up and ran out of the office. She burst into tears when she got outside the building. The counselor approached her and tried to comfort her. Renee spazzed out. "Get off of me! Get away from me! I want another test! God, please!"

She finally broke down and fell into the counselor's arms. Realizing that she had nowhere else to turn, she did the only thing she could do. She went back inside the building with the counselor.

Petie was shocked when Ladelle called him and told him what had happened to Lydia. "Didn't you have the TV on? It was live on all the news channels," Ladelle said.

"Nah, I ain't been watching that shit. I got tired of seeing my own face on TV," Petie replied. Ladelle told him that everything was okay with Lydia and that they were staying at his mother's house.

"I know for a fact that the same kid busted up my shit, too," Ladelle said after informing Petie about the Escalade. He told him that Lydia didn't want to stay in the apartment anymore.

"Listen, I'm gonna run into that cat in the system; I know them crackers are gonna run up on me any day now. It's been over two weeks, and my time is limited, dick," Petie said. They continued to talk, and Petie asked Ladelle if he'd heard from Renee; he hadn't spoken to her in over a week.

"I need to holla at you about something," Ladelle replied, not

giving Petie an answer. "Maybe we can meet up tonight. I wanna let you know about some things that went down before we got knocked."

"What you wanna holla at me about, dick? I mean, you talking to me like it's some life or death shit. What's really good?" Petie asked, wondering what the fuck he was talking about. Once again, Ladelle didn't answer Petie. They agreed to meet at the Carver houses later on that night.

Petie called Renee at Rhonda's house, but no one answered. He was tight about not being able to reach her. For almost the past two weeks, whenever he called, Rhonda would say she wasn't there.

Petie decided to drive to Manhattan. He put on his do-rag and baseball cap, hopped in his ride and headed toward the expressway.

Renee got home after leaving the clinic and was glad to see that no one was home. She needed time to herself to regroup. She had decided not to get re-tested immediately; maybe in the next three months. She wanted to go and see Share and she needed to talk to Petie. She was devastated.

Renee called Share's hospital room and was told she had been discharged. She called Venus and left a message on her voicemail. Finally she decided to call Petie.

"Where you been, ma? I'm on my way to the city," he said.

"For what?" Renee asked him. Petie could hear the attitude in her voice.

"What you mean *for what*? So I can see you—that's for what. What would make you say some shit like that?"

"Petie, I went to the clinic today and got my HIV test results. We really have to talk." Petie already knew what Renee wanted to talk about. He told her that he would meet her at Sylvia's and she agreed.

Renee hung up the phone and called the counselor at the clinic. She wanted to know where the support groups were and how she could get connected. She was still in shock after getting her results and finding out that she'd gotten the virus from Petie. She wondered if he knew he was positive. When she told him she'd been tested he hadn't said anything. He didn't seem surprised at all, and that bothered her. It made her think that maybe he knew all along. The thought made her sick to her stomach. She rushed to the bathroom and threw up.

Renee glanced down at the list of support groups that she had written down on a sheet of paper. Then she went to the kitchen to pour herself a cup of green tea. She had decided to change her whole diet. Everything had to change in order for her to stay healthy and live longer. And Renee had more to think about than just her own health; she had to think about Darnell and Dante's welfare, and she dreaded the thought of having to tell them. *How will they take the news? Will they still love me?* So many thoughts were going through her mind that her head started hurting. She got on her knees and prayed.

Renee looked forward to surrounding herself with other women who had the virus. She wanted to find out how they dealt

with the disease, and lived with it from day to day and still held on to their sanity.

Renee was totally disgusted with Petie, even by the sound of his voice. She couldn't wait to take her sons to go and live with her mother in Pennsylvania. She should have left Petie's ass years ago, she thought, but she chose not to for the sake of the boys. Now she had good reason to, but first she wanted him to know that she had met with Share and knew everything. Renee wanted Petie to know that she knew all about their erotic affair and that he attacked her after she told him she didn't want to be bothered anymore.

Renee hadn't loved Petie for years, and she had finally hit rock bottom with him. Enough was enough. And maybe if she'd left him years earlier, she wouldn't be infected now. She decided not to dwell on her diagnosis; what was done was done, and she had to keep herself healthy for the future.

Petie exited the freeway. He called Renee to tell her he'd see her in about twenty minutes.

"Yeah, all right," she said and hung up. Petie dreaded this day; he knew he'd be having this discussion with Renee sooner or later. He just didn't know when. He decided to act surprised and just as shocked as she was.

Petie had been tested for the virus six years earlier. Unable to accept the positive result he got tested three more times, and each time the outcome was the same. He kept it a secret from Renee, continuing to fuck her raw, not realizing that he was re-infecting himself. He just thought he was spreading the virus. Now Renee knew, and he planned to appear devastated by the news.

He called Ladelle to tell him that he was in the city. He'd swing by to see him after meeting with Renee.

Renee stepped out of the cab and went inside Sylvia's restaurant. She saw Petie, already seated at a table, and she joined him. He leaned across the table to kiss her and she turned away. He pretended not to be bothered by it and asked her what she wanted to eat.

"Nothing; this isn't a social dinner, Petie. What you think— I'm stupid?" Renee said reaching inside her pocketbook. She handed him a copy of her test results.

The waitress came and put a pitcher of water on the table. She asked them if they were ready to order. "No, not yet," Petie said, and when Renee turned her head he winked his eye at her.

"When you're ready to order let me know," the waitress said smiling at him.

Renee got right down to business. "I met Share and she told me everything." Petie pretended to be confused, like he didn't know what she was talking about.

"Who the fuck is Share?" he said, sounding so convincing that he almost believed he really *didn't* know her. Renee looked at him like he was crazy. Petie tried to speak, but she cut him off. She told him she knew all about the fucking in the ass, and how he got jealous over her new boyfriend and then went and shot up her restaurant.

"I went to see her in the hospital. How could you, you sorry

son of a bitch! You make me sick!" She rose up from the table, but Petie grabbed her arm and told her to sit back down. She pulled away from him and lowered herself back into her seat.

"Let me tell you about that grimy bitch," Petie said. "She'll say anything to see me and you have problems. That bitch said I attacked her? You know how many bitches I got throwin' the pussy at me? I *give* pussy away."

Renee leaned across the table and slapped him hard. "I hate you!" she shouted. Several patrons in the restaurant had now stopped eating their food to watch the scene.

Renee didn't have time to sit there and listen to the bullshit. She knew Petie was a lying ass. She got up from the table and left.

Petie followed her out of the restaurant. He told her he couldn't believe that she was siding with Share over him.

"Petie, p-l-e-e-e-a-se stop with all the lies. You're a no good son of a bitch, and I've always known that. I'm really mad at myself because I should have left you a long time ago. I just didn't want to take your sons away from you. I know how much they mean to you." Petie started to say something, but Renee continued on. "Shut up, damnit! I'm taking the boys and I'm leaving. I don't want them around you. You ruin lives, Petie, and I won't allow you to ruin theirs. I'll be damned if I let you corrupt them any more than you already have," she said and walked away. Petie stood there watching her for a moment, and then he bounced.

Chapter Thirty-seven

Kalif waited to see the judge. He was in a holding pen with other detainees who were also about to be arraigned.

At first he wouldn't go into the bullpen when the guards had taken off his handcuffs; the other detainees didn't look right to him. They all looked like worms with do-rags.

Kalif began to scream. "Aaaaaaahh...no! No! No!" The guards jumped back and looked at one another. Kalif continued to scream and hold his head. The niggas in the bullpen didn't know what the fuck was wrong with him. They didn't know that he was on his last dust trip.

The correction officers called for back-up to get Kalif inside the pen. His fingers were wrapped so tightly around the bars from the outside that they had to be pulled off one by one. The officers

finally got him inside the pen and slammed the gate shut behind him.

Kalif ran from corner to corner of the pen, screaming like a madman. Finally, he stopped in one corner and stood there with his back to the wall. *My God*, he thought. *Fucken aliens everywhere...do they have three feet?*

One of them was coming toward him now. Kalif started screaming like somebody had his balls in a vice grip. "Back the fuck up!! N-o-o-o-o!" he screamed in terror. The alien was saying something to him now, but he couldn't really hear him. All of the other aliens started to laugh. They didn't know what his malfunction was, and he screamed and yelled until the C.O.'s moved him to another cell.

Kalif curled up on the floor into a ball and wondered where all the aliens had come from. He wondered how long they had been on the planet and how many of them there were; they seemed to be everywhere. He bet that Lydia had called them on him. He was sure of it. He lay on the floor rocking, waiting for his name to be called.

Before seeing the judge, Kalif met with his attorney and was told what his charges were. He didn't understand what was going on. He didn't remember doing any of those things, and when the bailiff called his name and docket number, he jumped at the court officer when he walked up to take him to see the judge. That was the wrong thing to do; he was tackled to the floor and handcuffed so tightly that blood came out of his wrists.

The district attorney read off the charges against Kalif and asked that he be held without bail. Kalif's lawyer recommended that he undergo a psychiatric evaluation to determine his mental state.

The judge agreed, just based on Kalif's behavior in the courtroom. Kalif was taken back to the bullpen and waited to be transferred to Rikers.

Petie decided to get a hotel room and stay in the city instead of going back to Roz's place in Queens. He went to the Fame Hotel on 135th Street and got a room. He didn't care that the precinct was right down the block; nothing mattered anymore. Renee had him fucked up.

Petie got upstairs and laid his burner on the bed. He went into the bathroom and splashed water on his face. He looked at himself in the mirror and then wiped his face off with the towel that the rinky-dink hotel had provided.

It was early, and he still had to see Ladelle to find out what was too important to be discussed over the phone. He lay back on the bed and thought about everything that had happened since he'd come home. All this shit was Share's fault. She was the one who had started all this shit.

Petie was definitely in denial. He just couldn't stand the fact that Share had cut him off. Bitches didn't cut him off. He cut *them* off. It was Share's fault that there was a manhunt going on for him after being home for only two months. *If it ain't one thing it's another*, he thought.

He tried to call Renee at her sister's house, but she wouldn't come to the phone. Then he called Roz in Queens and told her he was going to rest in Manhattan for the night. "Keep your eyes

open, and make sure you make it back here safely—you hear me, baby boy?" she said.

"I will. Good lookin' out, ma—one." Petie snapped his cell phone shut. He had always been feeling Roz. She was a thorough-bred, and bitches weren't built like her anymore. Finally he dozed off.

His cell phone rang, waking him up. It was Ladelle, telling him to meet him by the water. Petie put the burner in his waist and locked the hotel door before taking the steps, two at a time, to go and meet him.

Ladelle was already parked, and Petie pulled up alongside him and got out of his truck. Ladelle did the same. He didn't waste any time; he dropped it like it was hot and told Petie about he and Renee.

Petie couldn't believe what he was hearing. "What the fuck you mean you and Renee was sexually involved? So you tellin' me you been fuckin' my wife, dick? What kind of shit is that?" he asked Ladelle, hoping that this was just a bad joke.

"Yo, Petie, man, I don't know what to say. I don't even know how the shit happened. It ain't like one day I woke up and decided I was going to fuck her. Nah, that's not how it happened. We been doing this for a minute." Petie looked at Ladelle, wondering if this was his best nigga standing before him or an imposter.

"So why you telling me this shit now? You could have kept that shit to yourself, dick."

"Because, after all the shit that done happened with Lydia being taken hostage, my unborn's life being put in danger and the gunplay at McDonald's, it was like a wake-up call. Fuck that, dick.

I'm trying to live right, and I think I owe it to myself and my unborn to get rid of the dirt in my life. I'm ready to give my life to God. You know what I'm sayin'?" Ladelle said, making a sincere effort to explain to Petie where he was coming from. Petie didn't say a word, and his back was to Ladelle now.

Before Ladelle could say anything else, Petie swung back around and put his burner in his face. "So you played me close all these years, and the whole time you was fuckin' my wife? Now you want to come clean and give your life to God? Aiight, cool, I'm gon' help you," Petie said and pulled the trigger. Luckily, for Ladelle, the safety was still on the gun. In an instant he smacked the gun out of Petie's hand. He tackled him to the ground and then punched him in the face. Petie head butted him, forcing him backwards. Ladelle jumped back on him and held him on the ground by his throat.

Ladelle was furious. "You put a gun to my head? You talkin' 'bout all the years we stomped together, and you put a fucken burner in my face, dick?! You was *never* my nigga, doin' some shit like that! I'd rather you fucked Lydia than put heat to my grill!" He released his grip from Petie's throat and then went and picked the gun up from off the ground. He threw it at Petie. "Do what you gon' do," he said. "You punk muthafucka!!"

Petie took the safety off the gun and pointed it at Ladelle. Ladelle looked at him and turned his back. He heard Petie cock the gun. "Yo, dick...dick!" Petie yelled out. Ladelle didn't turn around. He kept it moving and headed back to his mother's car. "Yo, La, act like you don't hear me and I'ma put two in your back!" Petie shouted.

"Do what you gon' do, my nigga. I'ma pray for you," Ladelle

said before pulling off.

Petie stood there with the burner in his hand. Ladelle's words had stung him like a bumble bee. Petie watched him drive out of sight without once looking back.

Chapter
Thirty-Eight

Petie got back in the Navigator and called Renee. Once again, her sister, Rhonda, told him that she refused to come to the phone. He wasn't trying to hear that. "Tell her to get on the phone before I pop up on the doorstep."

After a few minutes Renee got on the phone. "What is it, Petie?" she said.

"Who the fuck you wish was calling? Or should I say, who you *thought* was calling—maybe Ladelle? Huh, bitch? I'm talking to you! You would have *run* to the phone if it was Ladelle, right?"

Renee took a deep breath. "So he told you?" she said.

"What you think? *You* sure as hell didn't tell me!!" he hollered into his cell phone.

"Petie, what do you care? You haven't paid attention to me

in God knows how long. Does it really matter now?"

"Fucken right it matters, bitch!! How you sound askin' me a question like that?"

"I was lonely and needed some attention, and you were never around to give it to me. What do you suggest I should have done?"

"Not fuck my man, that's for sure!"

"You got some nerve!! You were out fucking anything in tight jeans, and you were never home!! Maybe if you were, I wouldn't be infected. Now you hold that!! And as far as your clothes go, I'll bring them to you. Other than that, we don't have anything to discuss— not now or when I bring you your shit. Now, this conversation is over!!" Renee slammed the phone down before Petie could say anything else. He threw the cell phone onto the passenger's seat and punched the steering wheel. Shit was closing in on him and he had nowhere to turn.

He headed back to the hotel to get some rest; maybe that would help him think a little clearer. He saw a cute chick about a block from the hotel and decided what he really needed right now— some pussy. Petie called her over to the driver's side of the truck. He could look at her and tell that she smoked. At this point in the game it didn't even matter. "What's up?" she said approaching him.

Your jaws, that's what's up, Petie thought. But instead he said, "You want to hang out?" He looked at her mouthpiece and concluded that she had the right goods. And after just a few seconds, he found out that she was with it. She walked around to the passenger side of the Navigator. When she got in, Petie asked her if she wanted to get something to smoke.

"Yeah, I can cop around the corner," she said. Petie parked the truck, gave her the money and waited for her to come back. He didn't care if she bounced with his dough and never came back; he had shit on the brain.

The chick returned and got back in the truck. "My name is Patrice," she said.

"Yeah, aiight, call me Ant," Petie replied. He wasn't interested in her name; he just wanted to know what her jaws felt like.

"Get in the tub and I'll be right back," Petie said to Patrice when they got to his hotel room. He locked the door behind him and ran down the steps and out onto the street. He went to the corner store and bought beer, cigarettes, soap, toothpaste and a toothbrush, and a douche for Patrice.

When Petie got back upstairs, Patrice was on the bed with her feet propped up on a couple of pillows. She lay spread eagle with the stem in her hands. Petie took a good look at her and saw that she wasn't too bad. She wasn't too fat or too skinny. He took the douche out of the bag he was carrying and passed it to her.

"You take it in the ass?" he asked her.

"Fa sho," she said. Petie knew they were going to get along just fine now. He took off his shirt and told her to go and douche out her ass. He watched her walk to the bathroom, her ass shaking like Jell-O. She didn't know that his butt-buster was already hard for her. He sat down on the bed, untied and removed his Timbs, and took off his jeans and boxers.

Patrice came out of the bathroom, and the look on her face

told Petie she was ready. Her eyes roamed his six-pack and the ana-conda between his legs. Petie was cut in all the right places with no body fat at all. He had the physique that all men want, and his tattoos made him look even more tempting.

Patrice fixed herself a hit and blew the smoke on his dick. Petie leaned back and began to stroke himself. "C'mon, ma, spit on me." She put him in her mouth and he moved her head up and down. She didn't have a deep throat, but she knew how to work her jaws. Des was still the best head nurse there was, as far as he was concerned. Patrice sucked his sides and licked his head until she tasted pre-cum in her mouth. Petie was good and brick.

Patrice got on all fours and moved to the end of the bed. She arched her back and threw her butt in the air. "Let me see what you workin' with," she said. Petie liked that. He knew he was going to have fun with her. He wet her asshole and slapped the tip of his dick on it. Then he applied pressure and entered her. She tried to move forward, but he pulled her back toward him. He lay on top of her and stroked her long and deep as she cried out. He liked her; she sounded like Share. The thought of Share made him mad, and he started to fuck Patrice harder. If he went any deeper, his balls would be in her ass, too.

Petie couldn't hold out anymore. He busted off, draining himself inside of Patrice's ass. He slid out of her and went to the bathroom to wash himself off as Patrice lay on the bed with her thumb in her mouth. *Just like Share*, he thought when he came out of the bathroom and looked at her. He had to admit it: Share had him bent.

"You aiight?" he asked Patrice.

"Yeah, I'm just tired," she said as she pulled the covers up over her and adjusted the pillows.

"Get some rest," Petie said. He turned on the TV and began to flick the channels with the remote that was on the nightstand next to the bed. He looked back at Patrice and saw that she had turned onto her side and was already going to sleep. Petie just sat in the chair and watched her as he thought about his next move.

When Petie woke up the next morning, he gave Patrice money to get them something to eat. He got in the shower after she left and thought about what he was going to do with her. He liked her, but she smoked crack and that was a no-no.

He was already out of the shower and getting dressed by the time Patrice got back to the room. He told her to be quiet while he called Renee. As usual, she didn't come to the phone. Rhonda told him that Renee said for him to turn himself in and stop calling her. He hung up the phone wanting to go over there and push her head into the wall.

He told Patrice to give him a number where he could reach her. She told him she didn't have a number, which didn't surprise him.

"Aiight, check this out: meet me back here tonight between nine-thirty and ten o' clock. We'll get another room." He paused for a few seconds. "Listen, no smoking tonight," he added. "We just gon' be on some Chuck Chill out shit".

"Okay, no problem," Patrice said. She didn't ask Petie for any money and he liked that. Most chicks who smoked always had their hand out. She didn't. He peeled back sixty dollars and handed it to her for her pocket. He told her to get her smoking out of the way now, because tonight it was a rizzie. He knew she'd be back; they always came back.

Petie and Patrice checked out of the room. After dropping her off, Petie called Roz and told her that he was on his way. So much pussy, so little time.

Chapter
Thirty-Nine

Renee woke up Darnell and Dante and got them ready for school. Darnell had begun to ask a lot of questions about his father. Renee didn't really know what to say; she never bad mouthed Petie to the boys and she wasn't about to start now. They meant the world to him, and that was the only thing she gave him credit for.

Renee called her mother in Pennsylvania to let her know about her diagnosis.

"Oh, Renee, I prayed when that epidemic hit that it wouldn't touch anybody I love. Good God, when did you find out?"

"Not too long ago, Mom. I'm scared. I don't know what to do or who to turn to. I just wanna die," Renee said on the verge of tears. She really didn't know where to begin, so she told her mother everything, starting with meeting Share. Renee and her mother were

best friends, so she felt more than comfortable telling her about Petie's infidelities. There were no secrets with them.

Her mother told her just what she wanted to hear; she told her to pack up and come home. Renee hung up the phone and cried, not only because her secret was safe with her mother, but mainly because she didn't turn her back on her.

Renee was ready to start a new life. She had only one more secret, but she thought it was best to keep it just that—a secret.

Share's nurse came and looked in on her. She was getting her stitches out in a couple of days and her body was healing slowly. Will was very supportive in spite of everything that had happened.

Share was lying down when Renee called her to see how she was doing. They talked about her diagnosis and Renee told her that she was also positive. They had bonded in such a short time under strained circumstances, and the way they communicated with one another made it seem like they knew each other much longer than they actually had. Renee told Share she was relocating to Pennsylvania and that she wanted to keep in touch with her.

"If there's anything I can do for you, please let me know," Share said. "Even if you need financial help, feel free to ask me for it."

Renee thanked Share for her offer and told her she appreciated her being so understanding, considering the circumstances. They talked a little while longer and agreed to stay in contact with each other no matter what. It was all good.

Renee brought Rhonda home with her to get some clothes and other things she needed. Renee wasn't surprised when she saw the police outside her apartment door. They approached her and asked if she knew her husband's whereabouts.

"No, I don't know where he's at and I don't care," she told them before putting her key in the door.

"Mrs. Mickens, can you give us a description of the vehicle he's driving?" one of the officers asked her.

"Sure I can. As a matter of fact, I even have a recent picture of the car." Renee went inside the apartment, came back out and gave the police a picture of the Navigator and the license plate number. They thanked her and got on their merry way. They actually already had a full description of his wheels; they had previously obtained the information from the Department of Motor Vehicles.

Renee and Rhonda put some clothes in a bag, and Renee packed some personal things for herself. She ran across an old picture of her sons with Ladelle and tears came to her eyes. She thought about Dante...the guilt was killing her.

Rhonda called her from the other room, bringing her out of her trance. "What you wanna do with this nigga's clothes?" she yelled out. Rhonda hadn't liked Petie from day one, and if it was up to her she would torch all of his shit.

"Just leave them where they are," Renee said. Her sister had told her that she would put all of her stuff in storage until she got herself situated.

"As far as his shit goes, I'm gonna throw it down the fucken

incinerator," she said, not minding Renee's request.

"No, I'm going to give him his clothes. He's going to need them...eventually," Renee said. They left in silence and went back to Rhonda's house.

Renee waited for her sons to come in from school so she could sit down and talk to them. She didn't know where to start. She wanted to tell them the truth, but she didn't want to look like the bad guy. However, she knew she needed to have a heart to heart with them so they would understand what was going on. Renee wanted them to know that Petie loved them to death, but they had to move on so they could have a better life. Dante would understand, but Darnell would put up a fight. Renee could hear his mouth already. She called her mother to find out about the schools and the job market in her area.

"Girl, don't worry about no job. That's not important right now. You just get out here, and we'll get the boys in school. Then you'll have time to get yourself employed. All right, baby?"

"Yes, Mom, you're right," Renee said before hanging up the phone. She began to cry like a baby. So much had happened in such a short time. She reflected on her life and realized that she had nothing to show for herself. Maybe Rhonda was right; years ago she had said Petie was the worst thing that ever happened to her.

As if she had been reading her thoughts, Rhonda came and hugged her and told her that everything was going to be all right. Renee held her close, and it was then that she knew everything would in fact be all right.

Venus sat at the kitchen table with a fifth of gin in front of her; she wasn't dealing well with BJ's death. She felt a loneliness that she hadn't felt in years, and she was angry. But she didn't exactly know with whom. She just knew that she was and the best thing to do was drink at the moment.

She really wanted to get at Annette...*that bitch*. What really got to Venus was how she came to the funeral and performed. *The nerve of her!* She couldn't wait to go to Annette's next court date, hoping that the judge would hit her in the head. Venus poured herself another drink, this time straight with no chaser. She'd be toasted before the night was up.

Venus called Share, and they spoke on the phone for hours about all the drama they had endured. Share told her to come over and spend the night; they could both use the company. Venus didn't really want to be alone, so she took her best friend's offer and told her she was on her way.

Chapter Forty

"Where you been?" Lydia asked Ladelle when he got home. He really wasn't in the mood to be answering any questions.

"I had to make a run. Everything is all right; don't worry yourself. I don't want you putting no stress on my unborn," he said as he rubbed her belly. She placed her hands over his as it moved across her stomach.

Ladelle was thinking about what had gone down between him and Petie. He wanted to talk about it, but not with Lydia. She wouldn't really understand, but there was no one else he could confide in. He thought about calling his mother but decided not to. He made up his mind to visit Lou's grave the following day and talk to him. Even though Lou couldn't talk back, Ladelle knew he'd be listening.... His whole team was dead behind Petie's dumb shit, and the nigga had the nerve to pull a gun on him. Ladelle wanted to forgive him, but he couldn't. The nigga had put a burner in his face and pulled the trigger. The only reason he was still alive was that the safety was on. Nah, he couldn't forgive that.

Ladelle thought back to when he and Petie first met. They were in the fourth grade and they had teamed up immediately. They did everything together. Petie was a wild child even then, and Ladelle chased the girls. Ladelle remembered how all Petie wanted to do was rob the other kids, while he just wanted to sneak in the girls' locker room. As the years went by, the two grew closer, calling themselves brothers.

Renee had moved into the neighborhood. She was friends with Ladelle's cousin, who introduced her to both he and Petie. Even though Ladelle was attracted to her, he stood by and let Petie claim her. One thing led to another, and Petie and Renee got engaged. They got married after she got pregnant with Darnell.

When Darnell was fourteen months old, Petie caught charges and went Upstate for two to four years. Renee and Ladelle began spending a lot of time together; he held her down while his man was up North.

Ladelle remembered how much Petie loved his son. All he talked about was his baby boy. Ladelle couldn't tell him that he was boning Renee while he was behind the wall. He knew it was foul, and he and Renee decided to keep it a secret.

Renee seemed to change after Dante was born. She always wanted Ladelle to be around. He didn't mind because they were like his nephews anyway. He had a special bond with them that could

never be taken away.

Ladelle was hurting. He had wanted Petie to know that he needed to change his life, and the only way he could get a fresh start was to clear his conscience. But Petie had taken it to another level. Ladelle thought that maybe he shouldn't have told him, but he thought it would be best if he heard it from him and not Renee.

Lydia called Ladelle to the phone. It was Renee, and she wasn't in a good mood. Ladelle was surprised by her call, but what surprised him even more was Lydia giving him the phone without beefing. But she knew what time it was and she had forgiven him. And she knew Renee wasn't a threat to her. Ladelle picked up the phone, wondering what she had to say to him. "Hello?" he said.

"Ladelle, all I want to know is why you found it necessary to tell Petie about us all of a sudden?" Renee asked getting right to the point.

"Because I needed to free myself of that bullshit. It was time to come clean and get that dirt out of my life," Ladelle said, hoping she'd understand. Lydia listened in on another line in the apartment, waiting to here what Renee had to say.

"Did it ever occur to you that lives would be affected when you decided to confess? Did you take the time to think about anybody else but yourself?"

"Listen, I already told you why I did it, and if you got a problem with that then I don't know what to tell you. This phone call is over. One," Ladelle said and hung up.

Lydia hung up her line and asked Ladelle what Petie said when he told him about his affair with Renee. "Does it really matter?"

he replied. Then he finally told her that Petie put a gun to his face before getting up and going to the window. Lydia could feel his pain. Ladelle knew he was wrong for fucking Renee, but he'd never put a burner in Petie's face under any circumstance. The whole shit was unbelievable, and he couldn't swallow it.

"I'm sorry, baby," Lydia said moving in close to him. "I understand how close you were with him, but sometimes we outgrow people. I know you're hurting and I know that was your man, but you've got to move on. Right now you've got to back up and let him go through what he has to go through to get where he needs to be. You've got to start living for your child."

Ladelle really wanted to forgive Petie, but he couldn't. He knew Lydia was right; he had to live for his unborn child. Ladelle started to cry like he hadn't cried in years. He said a silent prayer for Petie and one for himself.

chapter
Forty-one

Petie got back to Queens and called Rhonda's house. This time he asked to speak to Darnell.

Darnell came to the phone in a heartbeat. "What's up, Dad?" He hadn't spoken to Petie in a while, and he was happy to hear from him. "I miss you, Dad. When I'ma see you?"

"I miss you, too. Your mother's actin' like a real snowflake. She won't take my calls, and she's trying to keep me from seeing you," he said, knowing that he was planting a seed in Darnell's mind.

"Why she actin' like that, Dad? What's wrong with her?" Darnell asked. Petie knew Darnell was going to ride with him.

"I don't know. I think she's goin' through some kind of crisis. Listen to me, Darnell: no matter what your mother tells you, and I don't care what it is, always know that I love you to death—ya heard? No matter what, know that your father is a lieutenant. And don't let your mother turn you into no wuss. The streets is military, so you gotta be a soldier. And if anything happens to me you gotta take care of Dante, because he's soft like your mother. You hear me?" Petie said.

"Dad, why you talkin' like you're about to die or something? Stop talking like that; you're scaring me. Anyway, when am I gonna see you?"

Petie hated the fact that he hadn't seen his sons in weeks. The last time he saw Darnell was when he was in the hospital. "Soon," was all Petie could say. He really didn't know when he would see him again.

Darnell told Petie that every day all the kids at school talked about his picture being on TV. He said it kind of turned him into a celebrity. And he said that whenever he was asked about him, he'd just say, "Yeah, that's my dad. He 'bout it like that." Petie listened to Darnell and thought about how much he sounded like him. Damn, he wanted to be in his boys' lives so badly, but the way things were going he didn't know if he ever would.

"Where's your brother?" he asked Darnell.

"Outside with some girl from school," Darnell replied. Petie thought that maybe Dante wouldn't be a wuss after all.

Petie told Darnell that if he needed anything at all to call him, even to just talk. He could tell that Darnell didn't want to get off the phone, so he told him to call him tomorrow when he came in from school.

Darnell hung up the phone and went outside with Dante. He

didn't want to be in the house with his aunt, and he definitely didn't want to be around his mother. They were the enemy as far as he was concerned; anybody trying to keep his father away from him was an enemy.

Petie thought about the conversation he had with Darnell. He smiled to himself. He knew it was just a matter of time before Darnell flipped on Renee. He could see Darnell now, spazzin' out on her. Dante would turn on her eventually, but it would take some time.

He thought about Ladelle fucking Renee, and it no longer made him angry. Petie always knew Ladelle was a pussy playa, but he violated when he crossed that line. However, it wasn't like Ladelle had put a gun to her head and took it. Nah, that wasn't the case. Renee gave that shit up willingly. Now he knew why she hadn't been giving him any pussy.

Petie turned on the news and saw a picture of his Navigator plastered across the screen. He sat in shock as the reporter gave a full description of his vehicle along with the license plate number. *Oh shit*, he thought. They were closing in on him for real. He knew he'd be captured. It was just a matter of time.

He called Roz on her cell phone to tell her what he had just seen on the tube. She was in Jamaica with her peeps. Petie told her he was going to need a set of wheels quickly. Roz had all kinds of connections, so she could make that happen. "I bet your grimy-ass wife told the cops something for your shit to be on the news like that." Petie thought that maybe she was right.

"I don't think she would go out like that," he said trying to defend her, even though he didn't believe what he was saying.

Maybe she *would* do something like that, considering the way she had been acting lately.

"Oh, you don't think she'd do that? Well, then, why all of a sudden they got your shit on the air? I bet you a brick they threatened her and she sold you out. They applied some pressure and she broke," Roz said making a lot of sense to Petie.

Petie thought about Renee saying he should turn himself in and all that other bullshit he wasn't trying to hear. *Maybe she did sell me out. Who knows?* he thought.

"Yeah, you're probably right. But anyway, see about that car so I can get around."

"I'll make it happen. In the meantime, just be easy and stay in until I get back," Roz said.

"Aiight, but I gotta be in Manhattan by nine-thirty, so have shit together by then," Petie said before hanging up the phone. He had to meet Patrice back at the hotel, and he didn't want to miss her. She was a stress reliever. If his time wasn't limited, he would take her under his wing and mold her. She wouldn't be getting high anymore, fa sho. He hoped she showed up; he was feeling aggressive and wanted to beat something. He really wanted to be up in something right this second, and he decided to go outside and see if he could find the chick he had seen the last few days hanging around.

Petie was wearing his do-rag and a pair of Roz's sunglasses. He looked around, making sure the coast was clear. Then finally he saw her. He walked up to her and said, "Can I speak to you for a minute?"

"Who, me?" she said stopping in her tracks.

"No, your sister. Of course I'm talking to you; who else you see standing there?" She approached him slowly and he said, "Let's take a walk." They went over to a nearby building and waited for someone to come outside. When a man walked out, they went inside the building, took the elevator to the top floor and then went up to the roof. Petie pulled the python out on her.

"Where you gonna put that?" the chick asked. Petie went in his pocket and took out two dimes and gave them to her. He stood in front of her and stroked himself.

"Come on, ma, let's do this," he said. She pulled her pants down to her ankles and leaned over the railing. Petie spread her cheeks and didn't like what he saw. She also had bumps all over her legs, like roaches had bitten her. The skin between her thighs was wrinkled, and it looked like it needed to be ironed. He looked at her with disgust. He just wanted to get this over with. Without hesitating any further, he slid up in her.

When he pulled out, there was cottage cheese on his dick. It smelled like cat food that had been in the bowl for too long. "Let me see what your gums feel like," he said. She went to work, damn near sucking his skin off. Petie should have known she was a head nurse by the stretch marks around her mouth. He busted off and she swallowed it all. He gave her another dime and a dollar. "Forget my face and take that dollar and buy a douche," he said and bounced.

chapter Forty-Two

Roz came in around seven o'clock and gave Petie the keys to a white Chrysler 300M. It was fully loaded and had a full tank of gas. Petie was straight. Roz gave him the registration and insurance card, and she said she had some people who would take care of the Navigator. Petie told her to do her thing, and she made a phone call to have the ride picked up. They swung an episode, and she hopped in the shower right before Petie left to go and meet Patrice in Manhattan.

Renee and Dante were playing Scrabble when Darnell walked into the living room. He had an attitude, and he rolled his eyes so hard at Renee that she almost thought he was possessed.

"What's wrong with you, Darnell?" she asked him.

"Nothing," he said and flopped down onto the couch. Renee asked him again, and this time he answered her with even more attitude than the first time. "I *said* nothin'. How many times you gonna ask me?"

"All right, well, change your tone of voice so we don't have a misunderstanding—you hear me?"

"Whatever." Darnell sucked his teeth, got up and went to his room. Then he slammed the door behind him, locked it and turned on some loud music. Renee knocked on the door and when he didn't answer, she yelled out loudly, asking him to turn down the music. Darnell acted like he didn't hear her, and he turned up the music.

Renee never cursed at either of her sons, but she was ready to go ballistic on Darnell right now. He finally opened the door and asked her what she wanted. She looked at him like he was out of his mind.

"What do you mean *what do I want*? Who do you think you're talking to?"

"Nobody," he said and turned his back to her.

Renee wondered if he was getting high. "Darnell, are you doing drugs?" she asked.

"No, are you?" he replied. Renee could not figure out what his malfunction was, but she knew it had to be something serious. He had no right to be talking to her like this, and she wasn't going to stand for it any longer.

"Darnell, please tell me what's wrong. I don't like your attitude and your tone of voice is unacceptable. Now what is the problem?"

Darnell started to cry. He turned around to face her and said, "Why you tryin' to keep Dad from seeing us? I don't care what he did; he's still my father."

Renee hadn't seen Darnell cry like this since he was ten years old. She really didn't know what to say, and she needed to say the right thing now because she didn't want him to push her away any more than he already had. She understood his pain. Even when he was younger and Petie was locked up, he spoke to him every day. And no matter how far away Petie was, Renee always took the time to visit him with the boys. Darnell was not used to being away from Petie. That was the bottom line.

Renee sat him down and tried to explain that things had changed. They were going to move to Pennsylvania in order to have a better life. That's when Darnell flipped out.

"I'm not leaving my dad—you go! Me and Dante can stay with Uncle La," Darnell said, his mind made up.

Renee realized that she had to take control of the situation; it had clearly gotten out of hand. Now it was her turn to flip. "You don't tell me what you're going to do—I tell *you*! Do you understand me? Don't you ever think you're the boss, because you're not—*I* am!"

"No you not. My dad is, and don't you forget it!" he said rolling his eyes at her. Renee lost it and slapped him. She hadn't hit Darnell in years, and it was the last thing that either of them expected.

Darnell spazzed out and jumped in Renee's face. "You can't

be hittin' on me!" He wiped his tears, trying to be tough and continued. "Do you know how old I am?"

Dante walked into the room just as Darnell was storming out. He asked Renee what was wrong, and she told him that they were moving to Pennsylvania and Darnell hadn't taken the news too well. Dante went into the living room where Darnell was and told him to calm down. "Stop treating mommy like that," he said.

Darnell spazzed on him. He told Dante that their mother couldn't wait for their father to go to jail so she could kidnap them and take them far away. They wouldn't be able to visit him in jail at all either. He said she was a traitor, worse than Benedict Arnold.

Renee had heard everything Darnell just said. She walked into the living room and looked at him in disbelief. She was convinced that he was taking Ecstasy. She knew the pill was popular amongst teens, and now he must have started taking it too.

Dante was stuck in the middle, not knowing whose side to be on. He looked at them both and didn't know what to believe.

Renee began to yell, telling them why the police were looking for Petie, and Darnell yelled back at her and called her a liar. He grabbed his hoodie, went to the door and looked back at Dante. "You coming or what?" he said to him. Dante didn't move. Darnell told Dante to get his jacket and then he opened the door.

"Boy, you better *not* step out that door. Don't make me jump on you, Darnell. I don't know who told you that you couldn't get it. Now close that damn door!" Darnell remained standing there waiting for Dante until he finally grabbed his jacket and put on his baseball cap. He told Renee that he was sorry, and he left with Darnell. Renee ran over to Darnell and tried to grab him. He pushed her away like she was a mosquito. Renee fell back onto the carpet and Darnell slammed the door. The two boys ran down the hallway and Renee jumped up and opened the door. She stuck her head out into the hallway, yelling for them to come back.

When they reached the corner, Darnell went to a pay phone and called Petie.

"Speak," Petie said.

"Dad, she beatin' on us. You gotta come get us now," Darnell said exaggerating.

"What?! Who's beatin' on you?"

"Mom is. She just came in and started wildin' out on us. She was grabbing on me, and I had to push her down just to get out the house," Darnell said, being sure to tell just his side of the story. It really didn't matter, because either way Petie would have sided with Darnell over Renee anyway. He told him and Dante to wait right there; he was on his way.

Renee sat at the kitchen table, hoping that the boys would soon return. She started to call the police, but she really didn't want them in her business. She decided to call Rhonda at work to tell her what had happened.

After hanging up from Rhonda, Renee called Ladelle, thinking that the boys might call him. She could only hope that he would take her call. Renee told Lydia what happened, and Ladelle immediately came to the phone. "What you mean my nephews ran away? What did you do to them?" he said.

Renee started to ask him why she had to be the one to do

something, but she decided against it. She just gave him the details, and he told her he'd take a ride and see if they were heading toward his house. "Call me if you see them before I do," he said and hung up.

Chapter Forty-Three

Ladelle got in his mother's car and rode toward Rhonda's building. Renee had told him over the phone that she still wasn't ready to go home after Kalif had showed up at her door and wilded out.

Ladelle thought about Kalif for a moment. He had to give him credit; he was definitely 'bout it. But 'bout it or not, he was still a dead man if he ever got his hands on him.

Ladelle saw the boys when he got to Rhonda's block. He beeped his horn and waited for them to come over to where he was parked. Dante got into the car first. "Now tell me what happened," Ladelle asked Darnelle when he took a seat in the back.

Petie told Patrice he had to make a run and would be right back. She tried to keep him from leaving, not knowing that this was something he wasn't about to put off. But Petie wasn't surprised; all the chicks got open after they got the dick.

"Where you gotta go?" Patrice whined.

"To my sons. I'll be right back," he told her and went to put on his boxers. Patrice got up and followed behind him, snatching them out of his hand.

Petie flipped. "Check this out: anything dealing with my sons is more than important—ya heard? If I say I gotta get my sons, that means everything else stops. Don't get it fucked up!"

Patrice hadn't seen this side of Petie before. It was a side she didn't want to see again. He got dressed and said he'd be back as soon as he could, and he told her not to go anywhere.

Petie got to the spot where Darnell had told him to meet him and Dante, and he panicked when he didn't see them. He thought that maybe they went back inside the building. His cell phone rang. It was Ladelle, telling him that Darnell and Dante were at home with him. Petie didn't bother asking Ladelle how they ended up over there, because he knew that no matter what happened between them, Ladelle loved his sons like they were his.

Ladelle opened the door for Petie and invited him to come in and sit down. Petie told him he didn't want to, and he asked him where Darnell and Dante were. Ladelle told him that they were upstairs at his mother's house.

"So what kind of game you playing, dick? I ain't come to politic with you; I came to get my seeds," Petie said, grilling him the whole time.

"This ain't no game, punk," Ladelle said. "We need to talk, but not in front of my nephews. Fuck you talkin' 'bout?" Petie looked at Ladelle, and all the anger he was feeling had disappeared. He missed him. Ladelle was his man.

"Talk, nigga—I'm listening," Petie said before taking a seat. Ladelle started off with an apology, and he reminded Petie of all the years they had stomped together. He told him he forgave him for putting heat in his face, and if it was anybody else he would have killed them.

Chapter Forty-Four

Ladelle called upstairs to tell the boys to come down because Petie was there. They came downstairs, anxious to tell Petie what went down.

Darnell told Petie that Renee was funny style and he didn't want to be in the same house with her anymore." She talkin' about taking us out to Grandma's house. I'm not goin', Dad. I mean it. Me and Dante ain't bouncin' without you," he said, looking more serious than a chess player. Petie looked at Dante and asked him what he thought about all of this. Dante just shrugged his shoulders and said he would do whatever Darnell did.

Petie called Renee and told her that Darnell and Dante were at Ladelle's house with him. He paused for a moment. "Listen, you asking me too many questions. I said they're okay, and that's all that matters."

"Bring my sons home now or I'll come get them," Renee demanded. Petie wasn't feeling this shit at all and he got at her. He asked her what she meant by *her* sons, knowing that would piss her off even more. He told her that Darnell and Dante didn't want to be with her anymore because she was beating on them.

"What the hell you mean *beating* on them? Did they say they didn't want to be around me, or did *you* say that? Did you tell them their father is wanted for raping and assaulting a woman? Huh? Huh, punk?! Did you tell them that?! Do they know that their father is one of New York's most wanted?! Huh?!" she barked.

"Oh, shut the fuck up! You sound real stupid!" Petie said. Renee continued to holler and scream like somebody was trying to steal her purse, and Petie told her that she was going to bust an artery. Darnell stood behind him laughing. He might not have been if he could hear what his mother was saying on the other end of the phone. Petie told her he didn't have to tell them anything because channel 7 had already done that for him.

Renee got quiet; she must've forgotten that Petie's face was on the news every day. There was nothing the boys didn't know. Renee wanted to speak to them, but Darnell said he didn't want to come to the phone. Dante followed his brother's lead.

Ladelle and Petie sat and talked for a bit longer until Petie decided to take the boys home. When they got to the front of Rhonda's building, Petie told them not to give their mother a hard time and to be respectful. "She means well, so be easy on her," he said mainly looking at Darnell. "Call me every day and we'll meet up

after you get in from school."

"Aiight, Dad. But only 'cause *you* say so," Darnell said.

"Listen, if she asks you what I'm driving, tell her you don't know—ya heard?"

"See, Dad, you don't trust her either.... She might try and put something in our food," Darnell said before he and Dante got out of the car.

Petie waited until they got inside the building before pulling off. He drove back to the hotel.

Patrice was asleep when he got back. She didn't even hear him when he came into the room. Petie stood there and watched her as she slept, wishing he had met her earlier. She had potential; she was just one of those chicks who needed a chance to start over. She had shown him that she could follow instructions. That was important to Petie.

Petie's cell phone rang after he got undressed and turned on the TV. It was Roz. *Not now*, he thought. Petie hit the *No* button on his cell phone so the call would go to voicemail. He lay down next to Patrice on the bed, and she curled up close to him and asked him when he got back.

"That don't matter; I'm here now," he said grabbing her butt cheeks and spreading them. Patrice got on top of him and went to work. Petie pushed himself deep inside her and she rode him like a buffalo soldier. Patrice leaned forward and Petie sucked on her ear-lobe. He put two fingers in her butt hole as she continued to slide up and down on him. Petie was long and fat, and the way he had her ass spread open made her come immediately. He gently lifted her up and down, and her body shuddered until she finally fell on top of him, breathing heavily. Petie finger-fucked her ass until she came again and then he busted off, filling her insides with his juices.

Petie watched Patrice sleep. She was all curled up and looked real comfortable. She knew she was in good hands, even though they had just met a few days ago.

Petie really wasn't one for small talk, but he'd been wondering where Patrice was from; she didn't have a New York accent. "Baltimore, Maryland," she said after waking up.

"I knew you wasn't from New York by your accent," Petie said.

"Oh, a lot of people say that. I don't think my accent is that strong."

"Tell me how you started smokin' that shit. I know it was a knucklehead that got you started, right?" he asked, his question really more of a statement.

Patrice reached for her bag and pulled out some photos of herself before she started smoking. She was with some cat in some of them, and in others she was at a table counting money. Petie was impressed. He told her she looked real good before she started smoking, and if she really wanted to stop he'd help her.

Patrice got up from the bed. Petie noticed that there were tears in her eyes, and he knew she wasn't faking. He already knew she was in a lot of pain, just from her lifestyle alone.

Patrice was a dime piece. She just got caught up with a

knuckleheaded nigga who left her after she started getting high. She used to come to New York with the cat and re-up right uptown. And when she and Petie got to talking about shit, they realized that they knew the same people. The pictures revealed that she was doing her thing at one time and just got caught out there. Petie understood.

He went into the bathroom and took some tissue off the roll. He came back out and wiped Patrice's eyes. They sat at the foot of the bed now, and she turned toward him and put her head on his chest. She cried some more and told him how lonely she had been, and the only thing she could do for that loneliness was get high.

Chapter Forty-Five

Petie drove uptown to Washington Heights after speaking to Calderon. He told him he wanted some weight, but he had something else in mind.

He got to Calderon's building and whistled up at his window. Calderon buzzed him in, and Petie walked up two flights to his apartment. Calderon greeted him at the door, happy as ever to see him. He knew that whenever Petie came through he always spent dough.

Calderon went into the bedroom and came back out with the two bricks that Petie told him he wanted to cop from him. He offered to weigh it, but Petie told him it wasn't necessary.

"Yo, poppy, I'm seeing you on TV every day. You gotta be careful, 'cause they looking for you like crazy, my friend," he said. Petie hated that 'poppy' shit. He told Calderon that he was about to

bounce. He got up like he was pulling out his money, but instead he pulled out his burner. Calderon froze like water in an ice tray. "Poppy, what 'appen?" he asked Petie.

Petie looked at him and gave him a crooked smile. "Poppy this, nigga," he said before putting two in Calderon's chest and one in his head. Petie didn't think anybody else was in the apartment, but he walked through just to make sure.... Calderon, knowing that he was on the run, had trusted him enough to let him into his apartment while he was there alone with all that weight in the house—*dumb muthafucka.*

Petie put on a pair of gloves that were inside his jacket and ransacked the apartment. He took a kitchen knife out of the sink. He cut open the mattress in the bedroom and then he tore open the living room couch. There he found a bag of money, which he laid in the middle of the floor. When he cut open the sofa bed he found two more bricks. He put everything in a shopping bag and bounced.

Petie lucked out when he caught Calderon off guard like that; usually there would be like six cats in his crib. But Calderon had dealt with Petie so long that he trusted him. However, Petie would never have been able to pull that off in the daytime.

He got back to the hotel and paid for another day in the room he shared with Patrice. Then he rented another room, where he called Ladelle and left a message on his voicemail, telling him to come through, before going back to the other room with Patrice. She didn't know about the additional spot.

Peite's cell phone rang. It was Ladelle returning his call. He wanted to know what was up, and Petie told him he had something for him and that he needed to get there. Petie hung up before Ladelle could say anything else; too many questions weren't good. Ladelle knew he was at the Fame Hotel on 135th Street, so Petie just waited for him to call and say he was outside. He took a sack of money out of the bag and counted it up real quick. He counted eleven hundred dollars and then gave it to Patrice, telling her to put it in her pocketbook. Petie kissed her on the forehead and headed back to the other room he had rented.

He got to the other room and started counting up more money when his phone rang. It was Ladelle, telling him he was outside.

"Aiight, dick, listen: I'ma come down, but I need you to go to that store on the corner and see if they got a calculator—and bring me back a pack of cigarettes," Petie said before hanging up. Knowing Petie and what he might be up to, Ladelle thought twice about his request before making a move.

Petie gave Ladelle enough time to go to the store and come back before he went downstairs to meet him. The desk clerk wanted more money when he saw Ladelle about to go upstairs with Petie. Ladelle gave him thirty bucks.

When they got upstairs, Ladelle put the bag with the calculator and cigarettes in it on the table. Petie took out the calculator and sat on the bed. He pulled the bag with the goods in it from underneath the bed and took out the bricks. Ladelle asked him who he had hit and Petie told him.

"Oh, word? You hit Calderon at his crib?" Ladelle said, trying to appear normal.

Petie gave him a 'what you think' look and told him the money was rightfully theirs for all the years they had copped from those Germans. "Fuck those oiyes, dick. How many times we paid for a hundred grams, and when we got back it was only ninety-two or some foul shit like that?" Petie said.

"Yeah, you right...you definitely right about that," Ladelle said somberly. He was feeling totally guilty about being there now. He reluctantly sat down and started stacking the money in tens, twenties, fifties and one-hundred-dollar bills. He wished he could backtrack his steps and tell Petie he had something else to do. But he was here now....

"I got this chick upstairs in another room, so I'm gonna run up and check on her. Hold it down until I get back," Petie said before exiting the room. Aside from everything they had discussed, he was still suspicious of Patrice. He thought that maybe he shouldn't have given her that money, because it might kick up her shit. But at the same time he had to know if she could be trusted. If she couldn't be trusted with eleven hundred bucks, then she damn well couldn't be trusted with what he was about to share with her.

He opened the door not expecting to see her, but she was sitting up watching the news. She told him that they had just shown his picture. The look on her face made Petie feel that she was proud to be in the company of one of New York's most wanted. And he could tell that she wanted some dick, but he told her he was taking care of business and to get some rest because they were leaving tomorrow. "I need you to be on point," he added. She smiled and rubbed his manhood, thinking about how big he was, even when he was soft. Petie rubbed her shoulder and went back downstairs to rejoin Ladelle.

Share and Will were at the 125th Street restaurant for its re-opening. She had been in contact with the contractors the whole time during the renovation, and she was more than happy with the repairs; the restaurant looked even better than it did before. She was impressed with the new security system, and she decided that they could officially open the store back up tomorrow for business.

When Abdul had returned from vacation he was horrified when he heard what happened. He was devastated, and he still had not yet gotten over it.

Will drove downtown to another location that Share was interested in buying; this McDonald's was larger and in a busier section of the city. Their conversations these days were mainly based on the restaurants and business in general.

Share was anxious to find out Will's results. He had handled the news about her having the virus like a trooper. She wasn't really sure if she had contracted the virus from Petie. She wondered how many people he had infected and if he knew he had the virus and just didn't care enough about anybody to tell them. Then she wondered if people would be able to look at her and tell that she was infected. Finally she wondered if she and Will would be able to have kids. So many things were going through her mind that she couldn't think straight.

"Why you so quiet, ma. Penny for your thoughts," Will said

taking her out of her zone.

"I'm sorry, Will. I was just thinking about my health...I pray that your results are negative. Whatever you decide to do, I'll understand. I just want us to always be friends, and please know that I never meant to cause you any pain or grief," she said on the brink of tears. Will pulled the car over and put it in park.

"What, you plannin' on goin' somewhere?" Will said. "Because I already told you I'm not goin' nowhere—positive or negative. I told you that years ago, so don't think a nigga gon' run out on you now. Ride or die, ma. We in this for life."

Petie looked into Patrice's honey brown eyes. "I got you, ma," he said. "All you gotta do is follow my instructions. I'm gonna help you get your life back together, and maybe you can help me, too." He asked her if she had any family still living in Baltimore, and she told him that her mother and aunt were there. Petie looked at her and smiled. Then he did what he didn't normally do with women other than his wife—he kissed her on the lips, and he told her he was going to make a move so they could have some money. He said he was on the run and had to leave New York as soon as possible. He told her not to worry because he would take care of everything.

"You game or what?" he asked her.

"Of course—when we leaving?" Patrice said. Petie told her he was going to pay for the room for another day and then take care of his business before they bounced.

"Believe me when I tell you we gonna be all right. I got this.

Just don't go against the grain, and everything will fall in place. You hear me?"

"I'm with you, baby boy," Patrice said. She had been smoking for almost a year. And she had come across plenty of niggas who had gangsta written all over their face, but she had never spent this much time with any of them. She and Petie had spent just the last few days together and he already made her feel special. But what really got to her was when he told her that smoking crack was a dead issue. Most niggas tried to give it to her, but Petie was doing just the opposite. That really made her feel good.

Patrice's mother didn't know that she was smoking crack. That would have broken her heart, so Patrice just kept it to herself. She missed her mother, and it felt good to be able to call her and say, "Mom, I'm coming home."

Chapter Forty-Six

Venus sat at her desk waiting for the District Attorney to call her back. Annette had turned down their first offer and Venus was pushing the D.A. to put her ass on trial. *The nerve of that bitch*.

Venus locked her office door and then went and pulled a bottle out of her desk drawer; she was drinking more and more these days. She leaned back and felt the burn of the drink as she swallowed it. She reached for a can of Planters Peanuts and took another drink before someone knocked at the door. She didn't want to be disturbed right now. "Who is it?" she yelled out.

"It's Dre. Are you all right?" Andre said. *Damn, what does he want?* Venus thought as she got up to go and open the door. Andre stood there in an Armani suit and shoes. She didn't know if it was the liquor or he really just looked that damn good. Venus decided that it was both.

She invited Andre in to sit down. They had both been pro-moted at the bank, and they each had private offices now. The liquor bottle was visible on her desk, but Venus didn't care if he saw it. "What can I do for you, Andre?" she said grabbing a handful of peanuts from off her desk.

"Nothing, really. I just wanted to make sure you were okay. I know you're under a lot of stress, and I want you to know that I'm here for you," he replied sitting across from her. Venus thought he sounded really sincere and thanked him. "Come here. You look like you need a hug," he added standing back up.

Venus smiled and got up from her black leather chair and walked over to Andre. At first she just stood there, looking into his eyes. They were pretty, and she had never noticed them before. Andre cupped Venus' face in his hands and kissed her on the lips. He pulled back and studied her face, hoping her eyes told him that she wanted more—they did. Andre kissed Venus again with such passion this time that her knees buckled. *Is it the liquor, peanuts or the kiss?* she thought. She decided that it was the kiss.

Venus could feel Andre's hardness through his pants, and she placed her hand on his crotch to make sure that what she was feeling was real. *Oh, it's real all right*, she thought. He was packing a shotgun. The muscles in her pussycat started to jump and throb. She pulled away from him and went to lock the door. Then she came back and sat on her desk. She pulled off her shoes and slid off her pantyhose. Andre looked at her in disbelief. It didn't take long for him to figure out what time it was.

Venus, now in a bra and thong, closed the blinds and helped Andre out of his clothes. He let his pants and boxers drop down to the floor. *Wow!* Venus thought. BJ was big, but Andre was huge. And he had a pretty dick, the kind she liked to suck. Venus bent down in front of him and teased the head with her tongue. He ran his fingers through her hair and then he lifted her up off the floor. He kissed her as she wrapped her legs around his waist. Then he entered her and pinned her up against the wall before stroking the life out of her. She came immediately.

Andre put Venus down on the carpet and beat his head on her clit. He continued to enter and pull out of her, and he beat her clit some more until it was swollen. He entered her again, putting her legs up on his shoulders and putting his hands underneath her, spreading her ass. Venus came again and Andre came too, now. They lay there catching their breath.

Venus was embarrassed; she couldn't believe what she had just done. She went into the bathroom connected to her office and washed up. Then she cracked the door and peeked through it to ask Andre to pass her clothes to her; she didn't want him to see her naked, as if it mattered now. He handed them to her and got dressed.

Venus came out of the bathroom fully dressed now. "I'm sorry. I don't know what came over me. I am so embarrassed," she said.

"Don't be sorry. I'm not. Furthermore, I think it was long overdue," Andre said. "Come see me before you leave," he added before giving her a quick kiss on the lips.

Venus sat at her desk and thought about what just happened. She felt guilty about giving herself to someone so soon after BJ's death.... *I'm sorry, BJ, but I gotta move on... rest, baby.*

Share and Will decided to purchase the McDonald's downtown. She figured she could close the deal for $220,000.00, a quarter of a million at the most. It was a busy location, like her other two restaurants.

She and Will drove to her co-op on Seventy-Fourth Street and she checked her answering machine. There was a message from one of the detectives. He notified her that Petie was still at large and she could call the 32nd precinct if she needed to.

Share thought about Renee and decided to give her a call. Renee was more than happy to hear from her. Share told her that she was helping the police so Petie could be apprehended. She gave Renee the names of two support groups that she could join before relocating to Pennsylvania. Renee was grateful, although the counselor had already given her more than enough information on support groups. But more important than that, she was grateful to speak to someone who understood.

They hung up on a good note, and Share was pleased that Renee still wasn't holding anything against her. They were two women who'd met under fucked up circumstances. Their beef wasn't with each other but with Petie. They both understood that.

Share sat back and said a silent prayer. And she said a special prayer for Petie, asking God to help her forgive him and to have mercy on his soul.

Venus was in Andre's office waiting for him to get off the phone. She was wondering who he was talking to. She felt herself getting a little jealous. Andre must have seen the irritation on her face, and he cut his conversation short. "Okay, Mom, I'll be there Sunday for dinner." Venus felt silly. *Look at that*, she thought. *You're already assuming shit*. Andre hung up the phone and grabbed his attache briefcase before getting up from his desk. "Let's go," he said guiding Venus out the door.

"Where we going?" she asked with a big Gatorade smile across her face. Andre didn't answer, and they drove to his house in separate cars.

"Park your car and get in mine; we're going for a ride," Andre told Venus when they got there. She didn't dare ask again where they were going. She felt like a kid waiting for a surprise from her father.

They stopped at a red light and Andre leaned over and kissed her. "Relax, I only bite behind closed doors," he said winking his eye at her.

Petie couldn't sleep and his mind was racing. He and Ladelle had counted $152,000.00. Petie gave him thirty grand and two bricks. He kept the rest, but he'd give some of it to Renee for the boys.

Petie called Roz and told her he'd need ID, and he asked how long it would take her to get it. She told him to get a Polaroid picture and she would make it happen. Petie knew he could count on Roz for anything. She had more connects than dots. If she didn't have so much shit with her, Petie would gladly take her. But he was feeling Patrice now anyway.

He sat back in the chair and watched Patrice sleep. Yeah, Patrice was his new shorty and they needed each other. One day he might tell her about his condition, but for now he'd keep it a secret.

Petie continued to sit there and watch Patrice sleep. It reminded him of when he and Renee first started out; he would watch her sleep for hours. He felt like he was keeping shit safe while wifey and his sons slept. These thoughts made his heart hurt. No matter what happened, he would make sure that his sons were all right.

Patrice turned over in the bed and looked at Petie. "I can't sleep anymore. Come to bed." Petie got up from the chair, got in the bed and gave Patrice the business. They made love all through the night. Petie took his time with her. He'd been with her for three days now, and it seemed like three months. He was really feeling her. He had never felt this way about anyone so soon before, and it scared him. If she fucked up he would beat her down fa sho, but he tried not to think about that.... *Petie and Patrice—fuck Bonie and Clyde.*

Chapter Forty-seven

Renee woke up early. She didn't sleep much last night. She kept thinking about how Darnell was treating her and how quickly he and Dante had turned on her. She felt like she was losing them.

She went into the boys' room, woke up Darnell first and then Dante. She then went to the kitchen and made some eggs, turkey bacon and toast for them. Rhonda worked last night, so she would be coming in at any moment. Renee made enough for everyone.

Darnell showered and dressed. He came into the kitchen and gave Renee a hug. "I love you, Mom. I'm sorry," he said kissing her on the cheek.

Dante came into the kitchen a few minutes later and sat down to eat with Darnell. Renee soon joined them and they ate in silence until Dante broke the ice. "Mom, I'm not coming straight home after school; I'm going to play ball."

"Are you telling me or asking me?" Renee said.

"I'm asking," Dante replied.

"Okay, but after you come in and do your homework and change your clothes," Renee said.

"But Mom..."

"Dante, you heard what Mom said. And remember, Daddy told us not to give her a hard time," Darnell said firmly.

"My bad. I'm sorry, Mom," Dante said.

They all finished eating and Renee cleared the table as the boys left for school. She was thinking about Darnell saying that Petie had told them not to give her a hard time. She didn't know what to make of it. Petie was a good, responsible father. She couldn't take that away from him no matter what. She just wished he would stay out of trouble long enough to be in Darnell and Dante's lives. *Oh, well*, she thought. There were some things she had no control over, and that was one of them.

The phone rang while Renee was watching the news. *Who could be calling this early?* It was Petie, telling her he had to see her. It was about the boys; he knew she would listen then. He told her to meet him at Pan-Pan's so they could talk. Renee got dressed and headed to Pan-Pan's in a cab.

Petie patiently sat a block away in the Chrysler and watched Renee get out of the cab and enter the restaurant. He wanted to see if she was trying to set him up. He didn't trust her, especially after what Roz had said. He watched Renee sit down and then come back out and stand in front of the restaurant. Then she called him on

his cell phone. He told her to wait; he was on his way. He watched her go back inside and sit down.

Petie got out of the Chrysler and locked the door. He put his backpack over his shoulder and hailed a cab. He paid the driver to back up to the front of Pan Pan's. He got out of the cab and entered the restaurant. He spotted Renee sitting in a booth and went and joined her.

Renee looked stressed out. "There's fifty thousand dollars in this backpack," Petie said sitting it down next to her. "It's for my sons; don't spend a dime of it on you—ya heard? And stop talking shit to them about me, Renee. What goes on between me and you ain't got nothing to do with them. I want regular phone contact with them. I don't need to speak to you, but don't try and come between me and my little men—you'll lose." Before Renee could speak, Petie got up from the booth and bounced. He went outside and caught a cab back to the Chrysler and drove back up the block to the hotel.

Patrice was in the shower when Petie got back to the room. He had paid the desk clerk for another day, just in case Roz didn't have his new ID ready. He remembered her saying she needed a Polaroid picture.

Petie watched TV until Patrice came out of the shower. He gave her a thousand dollars and told her to go to 125th and buy herself some clothes, two cell phones and a Polaroid camera. Patrice didn't ask any questions; she just dressed and did what she was told to do.

Petie called Renee. She answered on the first ring. "I just wanted to make sure you got back in safely," he told her. "Now before you start asking me questions, don't bother. Just get my clothes together, and I'll meet you somewhere to pick them up. Pack up everything in the suitcases and make sure I got pictures of my men in there—ya heard me?"

"When and where do I meet you, Petie?" Renee asked. Petie liked that; she was keeping shit simple.

"As soon as possible at the Y on 135th up the block from where I just left you," Petie said.

"All right, I'll go back to the apartment and do it now. When I'm finished I'll call you," Renee said and hung up the phone.

Petie called Roz and told her he would see her in the afternoon. He told her he was heading down south and that he would need the ID today. "Don't worry, baby boy," she said.

Petie hung up the phone, lay on the bed and looked up at the ceiling. He had plans to see Darnell and Dante at their school. He figured he would go pick them up and put some money in their pockets. He wished he could take them with him, but he knew that was far from possible. Renee would make sure that they were all right. She was the best mother in the world as far as Petie was concerned. No matter what happened between them, he knew there was nothing he could say about her in that department. She lived her life for their sons ever since they were born. Petie gave her credit when it was due, and definitely when it came to their sons.

chapter
Forty-Eight

Ladelle woke up to go to work. He was anxious and hyped. He didn't tell Lydia about the money because he knew she would have started riffin, and he didn't want to hear it. He felt bad enough already. But he would put the money to good use. He just had to.

Ladelle kissed Lydia on the forehead and left her a note. *I love U. C U 2nite*, it read.

Ladelle got in a cab and headed toward midtown. He called the insurance agent who was handling his claim on the Escalade. The agent told him that it was damaged beyond repair and they were going to replace it. Ladelle wanted to know when; it had been over a month. That shit should have been taken care of immediately. The truck had full coverage. What was the hold-up?

The cab pulled up in front of Ladelle's job and dropped him

off. Some chick who worked in the area was standing outside smoking a cigarette. Ladelle knew she worked close by, but he didn't know exactly where and didn't care.

"Good morning," she said to him licking her top lip.

"Yeah, good morning," Ladelle replied. She put her cigarette out and followed him inside his building. Ladelle looked back at her. *Scram, will ya?* he thought.

"My name is Lisa—and you are?" she said giving him her sexiest come-fuck-me look.

"I am happily married with a baby on the way," Ladelle said watching the sexy look melt off her face.

"Congratulations," she said not really meaning it.

Beat it, Barbie, Ladelle thought. That's just what she looked like—fake hair, tons of makeup and showing too much skin. Ladelle never did like chicks like that. Without the makeup they looked like shit. He liked his chicks natural. He started to tell her to go and find a pole to dance on.

Ladelle got to work, punched in, changed into his cook uniform and got busy. He made small talk with the other cooks as he chopped up carrots, celery, onions and green peppers. He was hoping the day would go by quickly; he wanted to do some shopping for the baby and Lydia.

Venus and Andre arrived at his place after going on a boat ride on the Spirit of New York. There was a live band and everybody was on the dance floor. Venus never imagined that she'd be having this

much fun after BJ's death. Andre made her feel alive again.

Andre had a nice bachelor pad. Venus looked around for signs of another woman staying there. There were none—at least she didn't see any. She looked through his medicine cabinet for bobby pins, a douche, mascara, etcetera. *Maybe he's gay*. The thought terrified her.

She sat on the sofa bed and checked the time; they both had to go to work in the morning. Andre slowly came up behind her. He began massaging her shoulders and kissing the back of her neck. His touch felt so good, and Venus felt like years of tension was being oozed out of her.

She got up and took off her clothes, and Andre undressed as well. He walked her over to the bed and then turned on his stereo system. He put on a Keith Sweat CD. The speakers pumped *Nobody*, and Andre made love to her like *nobody* ever had. Venus used muscles that she didn't even know she had. They tumbled around on the bed, making love while Andre whispered sweet noth- ings in her ear...he was so big, and Venus prayed that he wasn't damaging her uterus. They came together, and Andre rolled over and reached for the remote to the CD player. *Twisted* now played as he prepared to get in the shower. Venus dozed off, still hearing Andre's voice in her ear and feeling his hands on her body. She really *was* twisted.

Andre awakened Venus. He had made a light breakfast for the two of them and was getting ready for work. Venus tried to focus; she wasn't used to waking up in somebody else's bed.

Andre brought her breakfast in bed. "You look so beautiful in the morning," he said.

"It's too early to be telling lies, Dre. But thank you," Venus said. She started fixing her hair...God, she hadn't even brushed her teeth. She bit into a raisin bagel and drank some coffee.

Andre finished his breakfast and gave his keys to Venus. "Lock the door, and I'll see you at work. I gotta go to that meeting this morning." Venus knew what meeting he was talking about. If he waited for her he'd be late.

"All right, drive safely. I gotta go home and change clothes," she said before locking the door behind him. Now that he was gone, she had the opportunity to really snoop around.

Venus looked through his drawers and his mail. There was no indication that he was involved with someone else. Andre was too good to be true. She found his social security card and birth certificate and decided to run a check on him. She knew Share ran background checks on people all the time, and she would let her do it.

Venus got home, showered and changed. Bullet and Diamond had both given her a 'why are you just getting in?' look. She let them out the back door, filled their bowls up with food and headed out to work. She put on the headphone to her cell as she drove through traffic and called Share.

It seemed as if they hadn't seen each other in ages. Share told Venus about the restaurant she was going to buy downtown, and Venus told Share about Andre, hoping she'd be happy for her. She was, even if it was so soon after BJ's death.

"It's not like you don't know Andre; you've worked with him for the longest," Share said when Venus asked her to run a back-

ground check on him. Venus thought Andre just seemed so perfect and there had to be something wrong with him. Share didn't understand Venus' paranoia, but she took down his information anyway.

Venus got to work and checked her voicemail. She had half a dozen messages. BJ's aunt had phoned her, and the rest were business calls.

Venus returned the District Attorney's call immediately. He told her that Annette's lawyer was trying to cut a deal and have the charges reduced to a lesser crime. He said the chances of that happening were slim to none. They were closer to none actually, because Annette's pregnancy test showed that she wasn't pregnant at all. She had also failed a polygraph test.

The District Attorney's office was ready to charge Annette with second degree murder if she didn't cop out. Venus was very pleased with his work, and she wanted to be present when Annette got sentenced.

Venus hung up from the D.A. and called BJ's aunt to tell her the good news. They agreed to be at the trial every day if it came to that.

Venus ended their call and sat back in her leather chair. She remembered her and Andre doing the damn thing right there on the office carpet. She laughed out loud to herself as their episode continued to run through her mind.

Chapter Forty-Nine

Kalif was being detained at Riker's Island to be evaluated by two psychiatrists. His lawyer told him not to cop out because he had a good chance of beating the case. Kalif didn't believe him. He wasn't sure he trusted the Ritz Cracker.

His lawyer also said that since he was under the influence of PCP at the time of his crime, he wasn't responsible for his actions. Kalif understood that; when they told him he had hung a baby out of a window by one arm he was shocked, so maybe the cracker-ass lawyer could be trusted a little bit.

It was chow time, and Kalif wasn't for eating any mess hall food. He'd gotten arrested with a couple hundred in his pocket, so his commissary was all right—not to mention that LeRoy and Derek had set him out since he had been down.

Some kid asked Kalif if he was going to eat; he wanted to know if he could have his tray if he wasn't. "Sure, no doubt; you can have my tray," Kalif said and went to wait in line. When he got his food, he walked up to the kid who had wanted his tray and smacked him with it. The kid fell, and Kalif stomped him until some other cats pulled him off of him. Nobody really knew what had happened, because the shit jumped off so quickly.

"I'ma see you, punk!" the kid jumped up and yelled.

Kalif didn't take too kindly to threats. "See me now, you twinkie-ass nigga," he said and snatched the kid up again. Kalif beat him down until the CO's finally stepped in, put him in handcuffs and took him to the clinic. He didn't understand why he was being taken to the clinic; he wasn't the one who was hurt—the other kid was. He lay there bleeding while the other niggas just stood around, laughing and cracking jokes.

Niggas knew Kalif's style from the streets, and his dead brother's reputation gave him even more status. The inmates sat and ate now, talking about his jump-off and how quickly he had snuffed that kid. Kalif knew what he was doing; he was giving them something to talk about.

Kalif, now back from the clinic, sat in his cell eating potato-stix and a turkey sandwich. When he was done, he went to the phone and called Will. He told him what the lawyer had said and the date of his next court appearance. Will told Kalif that he, along with LeRoy and Derek, would be there. Kalif's phone time ran out, and he went back to his cell.

Kalif's lawyer wanted his case to be treated as a high profile one. "Fuck that shit!" was Kalif's response. "House me in G.P. with my niggas." His lawyer went on and on about how the judge had ordered that he be housed separately and there was nothing that could be done. Kalif settled for the 911 building with the inmates under mental observation. Half of them weren't M.O. anyway.

Kalif was in his cell reading when Ladelle crossed his mind. He was amongst the angry crowd that had attacked him on the day of his arrest; he had snuffed him as he was being brought out of the building. Kalif would never forget that scene or Ladelle's face, no matter how long it took him to get home. He had marked Ladelle for death.... *Beef never dies, you punk muthafucka,* he thought as he closed the book he was reading.

Petie left the bricks in the room with Patrice. Ladelle was gone now, and it didn't make sense for him to continue to pay for the other room. He didn't want to leave two kilos in an empty room with nobody to watch it. Besides, he didn't trust the old people at the desk; maybe they'd want to go in there and snoop around.

Petie told Patrice that he had something to put away in the room. He'd leave it a certain way so if she touched it, he'd know. It wasn't the only way he could find out if he could trust her, but hopefully she passed the test. If she didn't, he'd put a bullet in her and leave her ass on the roof.

Petie left the hotel and went to Roz's house. He gave her the Polaroid pictures that she needed to make up his ID. She left him at her crib and got on her job immediately, calling her connects. She had told Petie that she had somebody move the Navigator, strip and burn it and leave it in Brooklyn. Petie had never thought about that. It was a good thing that Roz did.

Petie waited for her to call the house and say she was on her way back, but she never did. He had forgotten to give her the numbers to his two pre-paid cell phones before she left. "Who's number you calling me from?" she said when he called her from one of the phones. She hadn't recognized it when it showed up on her caller ID.

"My new phone, ma. I forgot to tell you before you left. Listen, how long that shit gon' take? I wanna be on the road tonight," Petie said itching to get out of there. The vibe in her place didn't feel right anymore. He was paranoid, and he thought that at any minute the door would be kicked in.

He sat on the couch holding the burner, cocked and ready. Fuck it. If po-po came through the door, they'd better be ready to eat bullets.

Patrice was wondering what Petie had stashed in the drawer. Although he had told her not to touch anything, she had to know. She opened the drawer and saw a pillowcase. She took it out of the drawer and unzipped it. She couldn't believe what she saw—two kilos. There were knots in her stomach now, and she felt like she had to take a shit. That had always happened to her when she felt the urge to get high.

Patrice stood there staring at the material, and her mind began to race. She asked God to remove the thoughts and feelings that were overwhelming her. *God is good all the time*. The feeling passed and she put the bricks back in the drawer. She had been with Petie for four days now, and she was feeling him for real. She didn't want to give him any reason not to trust her. Petie had treated her well ever since picking her up that night.

When he put that thousand dollars in her hand, she thought about bouncing then. But her mother always told her that if she did people wrong, nothing good would come to her; so no matter how much crack she smoked, she never violated. She never gave a nigga a reason to hunt her down. Bad enough she was smoking; she didn't want to have to walk in fear, worrying about some niggas running up on her. She didn't violate unless a nigga gave her reason to.

Patrice was sitting on the hotel steps when Petie got back. "What you doing out here?" he asked. "I thought I told you I didn't want you in the streets unless I was with you. Get upstairs." They went inside the hotel and Patrice walked up the stairs behind Petie. He had *G* written all over him, and she loved it. She loved the way he laid shit down. He was the boss.

Petie went right to the drawer. There weren't any signs that his shit had been touched, but Patrice told him about finding it anyway. He didn't say anything. Patrice knew that was a good sign.

Petie had stopped off at a restaurant on his way back to the hotel. They sat on the bed and ate, talking about their trip tomorrow and what roads they were going to take to avoid the state troopers who'd be on the turnpike, trying to catch drug traffickers.

chapter Fifty

Petie sat in the chair with his burner on the table and watched Patrice sleep. She was all right in his book; he had a feeling that she had touched the material when he checked it, but she told on herself, which earned her some stripes. He had acted like he didn't know, hoping she'd tell him before he went ballistic, and she did. She had proven herself trustworthy.

Petie gave Patrice money to go shopping, and she came back with all the right things. He liked the dread wig she had bought; it would definitely give him a different look. She had covered bases that he hadn't even thought of.

Roz came through with all the ID Petie needed. He now had a new birth certificate, social security card and photo ID. She had done right by him, so he gave her a thousand dollars for keeping it real.

Renee would bring him his clothes in the morning. She would have the boys with her so Petie could see them before he bounced.

Petie got in the bed to get some sleep. Patrice eased up next to him and started biting his chin, which made him brick like cement. *A man's job is never done*, he thought. Patrice got on top of him and rode them both to sleep.

Renee lay in bed, thinking back to the time when Petie made her so happy that her heart smiled day and night. Now he only made it hurt, and she coudn't bear it. She had packed the clothes he wanted in a Coach suitcase and she'd be bringing them to him in the morning.

She wondered who he was laying up with; she knew he had *some* chick in his company. Petie was still a dime piece, despite all the fucked up shit he had done. She had spent sixteen years with him, and the only thing she had to show for it was HIV. *No, that's not true,* she said to herself. *I still have Darnell and Dante.*

She thought about her plans to move to Pennsylvania. She'd look for a job immediately when she got there, even though her mother told her she wouldn't have to worry about that. Her main concern was making sure that Darnell and Dante got into school that first week.

Renee was excited about starting a new life in a new state. Maybe she'd meet somebody there—someone the opposite of Petie...no more thugs and bad boys for her; Petie had been enough.

She wanted a nerd the next time around—maybe even a hillbilly. She said her prayers and went to sleep, thinking about a better future for her and her sons.

Petie woke up bright and early and called Ladelle, who was already up and ready for work. Ladelle told him to call him as soon as he got situated in his new spot.

Petie called Renee and told her to meet him at the Y on 135th Street. Then he woke Patrice up and got right in the shower; he had to leave in thirty minutes. She came into the bathroom and washed his back.

Petie got out of the shower and Patrice got in right after him. He got dressed and waited for Renee to call. Patrice came out of the bathroom and began putting on baby oil while Petie combed her hair. This was something new for him and it made him smile. The only time he had ever touched her hair was when he was pulling it.

Petie took the bottle of baby oil and rubbed some on Patrice's back. Soon she was at the edge of the bed on all fours. She couldn't get enough of the dick. Too bad she didn't know it was a sick dick.

Petie slid up into Patrice's kitty cat and she began to purr. She told him to open up her ass and give her the woodwork. He did as he was told; he took his dick out of her pussy and slid up in her bumper. He was rocking her so good that she started pulling her own hair. It was getting good when his cell phone rang. It was Renee, telling him that she and the boys were at the Y. He told Patrice to get dressed, so that when he came back they could just bounce. "Take everything out to the car and make sure we don't leave nothing here," he told her before leaving to meet Renee.

Reneee, Darnell and Dante were standing in front of the Y waiting for Petie. He walked up and hugged the boys, and then he pulled them to the side. He gave each of them a thousand dollars and they put the money in their pockets. Petie gave Darnell his new cell phone number and told him to call every day. Darnell got teary eyed and told Petie that he wanted to go with him. Petie explained that he had too much going on to take him and Dante along. Darnell looked at Renee like it was her fault.

Petie stood before Renee now. He told her that no matter what had happened between them, he loved her to death and she was still wifey. Renee started to cry, and she told him she wished things would have turned out differently for them.

Petie put them all in a cab and walked back to the hotel with his suitcases. Patrice was waiting for him in the car. He asked her where she had put the material, and she leaned back in the passenger seat. "How many months do I look?" she asked. *That's what's up*, he thought. She even had the transportation covered.

Petie put the keys in the ignition and started the car. He leaned over and kissed Patrice. "Let's be out," he said, and they headed for the George Washington Bridge. It was a wrap for New York.... Look out, Baltimore, Maryland. H-e-e-e-re comes Petie!

Sharron Doyle (right) and her mother (left)

Biography

Sharron Doyle is a hardworking writer from New York City. She wrote four titles while incarcerated. Her debut titled, If It Ain't One Thing It's Another, hit stores spring 07. Sharron stays busy in Harlem searching to write the perfect novel. Trini is her nickname. Ms. Doyle is proud of her Trinidad and Tobago roots. She lists her mother as a strong influence in her life. "I feel like I can take it to any level I want to, when I'm on top of my writing game."